NOAH'S STORY

Close Enough to Kill Series Novella

JACQUELINE SIMON GUNN

This book is a work of fiction. All names, characters and events are from the author's imagination. Locations are used fictitiously. Any similarity to actual persons, living or dead, is purely coincidental and not intended by the author.

Copyright © 2017 Jacqueline Simon Gunn
Noah's Story
By Jacqueline Simon Gunn
All rights reserved. No portion of this book may be reproduced by any process or technique without written permission from the copyright holder.

ISBN: 1546944206
ISBN 13: 9781546944201

FOR JOE

"There are some secrets which do not permit themselves to be told."

— *Edgar Allan Poe*

CHAPTER 1

Impossible. Mother was impossible.

"Mother. Please – " Noah said, exasperated.

"You must listen to me. Women always want to marry a doctor. You mustn't fall prey to the seduction of a woman who only wants you for *our* money. You must choose someone like Mother. A woman of means and integrity."

"But Mother, no one is ever good enough for you."

"Come. Go out with Lillian one more time. Mother likes *her*."

"But *I* don't."

"Just one more time. You haven't even given her a chance. I've exhausted myself finding you a woman worthy of our time. Listen to Mother."

Mother exhausting herself, now that's hilarious.

Noah sunk into his sofa and glanced at his mother's pictures on the side table. Five framed photos, all of Mother. A phony smile on ruby lips and piercing brown eyes poked at him through the glass. Those pictures mocked him as though mother were there, in his apartment, watching him. She insisted he have pictures of her throughout the brownstone.

He indulged her, because not indulging Mother was never wise.

Disgusted, he took a heavy breath, then turned all of her pictures face down.

Satisfied with his rebellion, he folded his arms across his chest. His lips twisted into a righteous angry scowl.

"Fine. One more date. But that's it, Mother. That's it. One more time. I mean it." He responded, sounding cautiously indignant.

"OK. Call her now. She's on call at the hospital. You know how hard residency is. I'm sure she could use a relaxing dinner."

"I'm sure."

"I will see you for our dinner tonight."

"OK. Bye."

Noah hung up, irritated, a sour look on his face. Only 8:00 a.m., and already his mother managed to stress him out. Not unusual. His mother, Belle Donovan, made a hawk seem docile. The woman epitomized overbearing.

He hopped in the shower, stayed in there for almost half an hour and tried to scrub the dirty sensation off of his skin. Even with the loofah and exfoliating soap, he still felt the grime. He scrubbed harder. The tingling that lingered under his skin felt like dirt, the result of his mother's inappropriate meddling. It had to be cleansed. He poured the exfoliating soap directly onto his chest and rubbed his skin with the tips of his fingers in short, rapid strokes.

Lillian Seasons was homely, a thirty-year-old brunette with pock-marked skin and a scrawny shapeless figure. He couldn't see himself ever being attracted to her. A week ago, at Mother's cajoling, he took Lillian for a drink. A daughter of one of Mother's friends from her spa, Mother insisted Noah would like her.

He gave it a shot, mostly to assuage Mother. He never liked the women she fixed him up with. They were always ugly, dull wallflowers.

Lillian's voice had a high-pitched tone. Dogs around the city could probably hear her squeal from a mile away. He would buy earplugs before he took her to dinner.

He would use them when he saw Mother, too, a buffer between him and her constant barrage of questions.

Since he was a young boy, Mother had always said: "Most women are sluts who only want you for our money. You must listen to mother. You are naïve. I don't want you to be taken and manipulated by a vile woman. Mother is only trying to help." Mother's voice sounded mellifluous whenever she said it, so as a young boy, he believed her. But as Noah got older, he recognized that her smooth, soft tone concealed a sly antipathy. Besides, Mother had shared her secret with him, a secret that made it hard for Noah to disregard the viciousness veiled beneath her elegant, "upstanding member of society and loving mother" persona.

He would never be attracted to anyone Mother approved of, he eventually decided. Another duplicitous ploy of Mother's to keep him single and available to live his life catering to her every whim. Either that or she hoped he would marry someone ugly, as homely as Lillian Seasons, maybe worse. Meanwhile, Mother was stunning and always impeccably dressed. She took advantage of every latest lotion and potion on the market to retain her beauty. And it worked, her regimen belying her real age by twenty years, making her appear a more youthful fortysomething. People kindly mistook her for Noah's older sister. How she would laugh with glee when they said that. No, Mother did not want to be replaced. She would never want him with a woman more attractive than she — or as attractive. Noooo… Mother could not have that.

He went into his fridge. No coffee. Annoyed, he threw on jeans and a sweater, left to grab a coffee and bagel at the coffee shop on Second Avenue, just far enough away from Mother's apartment that he wouldn't risk bumping into her. Mother never went east of Lexington Avenue.

Thank goodness for the little things in life. Although, knowing there was a part of the city Mother would never be in was not a little thing.

October, and the weather was perfect in the city. Blue sky, full sun, a crisp bite. He felt better as soon as he sauntered his way to the coffee shop in the fresh air.

The line was long when he arrived. Saturday morning, a little after 9 a.m., and the coffee shop was packed. Heavy eyes, yawning mouths, and tousled hair filled the small space. People looked like they had just rolled out of bed as they waited with excited desperation for their morning fix.

He sighed as he got in line. He had plans with Yvonne at noon. He had promised to take her to an exhibit at the Metropolitan Museum of Art. He looked at his watch, impatient to move on with his morning. He had hoped to get paperwork done before they met up, but the eternal line seemed to have other plans.

He tapped his foot, checked his email on his phone, tapped his foot some more. The line inched up. A woman in front of him turned to look out the door. Long dark hair, tall and thin, but curvy, too. From her profile, she looked striking.

Bored and needing a distraction, he decided to strike up a conversation. "Long line," he said casually to the woman.

She puffed out a breath of frustration. "Uh, yeah." She sounded as annoyed as he felt.

"I usually make my coffee at home. Ran out this morning."

She turned. "I dropped mine all over my kitchen." She said with a perturbed tone. Her lips made a thin smile.

The woman had the greenest eyes he had ever seen. Two emeralds shining back at him. They held a deep intensity, like there were layers upon layers of thoughts hidden back there. She also exuded a confidence, almost cocky, but not quite. Her jeans were ripped; her sweater seemed restless hanging off her shoulders, like it resisted when she put it on and was waiting for the right moment to bare her shoulders to the world. Something about her was terribly alluring.

"What a mess." He chuckled.

"It was." She turned back around.

"So what do you do?"

She craned her neck to answer him, but kept her body facing front. "I'm a graduate student."

"What are you studying?"

"Forensic psychology at John Jay College."

"How cool is that. A buddy of mine went to John Jay. He went on to law school afterward."

He observed her body language as she turned to face him. Finally, he had gotten her attention.

"I'm getting my doctorate. I'm studying criminality. I'm less interested in the law end of forensics. More interested in the psychology of the criminal mind. I'm thinking of doing some sort of investigative work. Or maybe just research. That's what I'm doing now. What about you?"

"I'm a medical doctor."

"What kind?" Her eyes studied him.

"An internist. I'm in a group practice, a few blocks away."

"Cool," she looked him up and down. "You working today?"

"No. I live a few blocks away too."

"I live around the corner."

"Are you from here?"

"Edgewater, New Jersey. But I've lived in the city since college. You?"

"I moved here when I was ten. Lived here ever since." He stuck his hand out. "I'm Noah."

"Kadee. With a D." She shook his hand.

"Nice to meet you, Ka**dee,**" he punched the "D" in her name when he said it, "with a D."

"Large coffee." Kadee ordered. Finally, they made it to the front of the line.

She reached for her money.

"I'll get that." He insisted.

"No. Thank you. Really it's not – "

"I insist." He brushed her shoulder with his hand and smiled. "Gotta help out the starving student."

"Alright. Thank you, then."

He kept asking her questions, wanting to keep her engaged in conversation. Although he sensed her guardedness, he felt her becoming more open. A couple got up from a nearby table, he glanced at the table and then at Kadee. They walked over, sat down. He could not believe how appealing she was. The dark hair, the green eyes, her taut curvy body, all attracted him, but her edgy, unconventional qualities were what roused his interest.

Definitely not the type of woman who made it easy to get to know, and Noah delighted in the idea of finding a way to break her down. Sensuous and intense, he wanted to peel back the layers of Kadee with a D, and find out what was underneath.

She talked and he observed the way her lips puckered slightly while she thought of what she wanted to say. Her eyes were emotive; he could tell she felt things deeply. Yet, she had this wall of self-possession, a barrier that hollered, *you're going to have to earn the right to know me.*

Figuring out a way to get beneath the surface of this woman enticed him. So, he continued to ask questions, nothing he was really interested in knowing. It was simply a way to get her to think he wanted to know things. Having to manage Mother his whole life left him with the uncanny ability to both detach and maneuver the complexity of the female gender.

That was not insignificant. In fact, if a man was to survive life without being swallowed whole by a conniving woman, understanding the female gender was essential.

Kadee stopped a few times and said, "Tell me about you?" She planted her pointer finger on her lip and waited for him to disclose something about him. But he knew better than to tell her too much. He gave her a generous smile and responded, "My life is not that interesting. I'd rather hear about you."

That always worked.

How many dates had he been on when the woman would go on and on about how the guys in New York City only talked about themselves. These dates, veritable information gathering sessions: a way for Noah to better understand what went on in the mind of women.

Mother both warned him about the dangers of women and set an example she insisted he follow.

About a half hour later, he felt the vibration of his phone. "Excuse me," he said to Kadee as he checked his phone. A text message from Yvonne: *Can we meet at 11:30 instead?*

"I'm running to the bathroom," Kadee said.

"OK." Noah smiled. He watched her ass as she walked away. Man, Kadee was sexy. Sitting back into his chair, he observed the swing of her rounded hips until she disappeared into the bathroom.

He loosened the neck of his sweater, then texted Yvonne back: *OK. See you then.*

When Kadee returned, she sat on the edge of her chair, smiled, said, "I have to get going. I'm meeting my friend downtown."

He felt the whisk of her body brush along his, and he knew she wanted him to ask for her number. Her eyes smiled. That was always a sign of women's interest in a man. Differentiating between the lip smile and the full countenance smile was a sure-fire way to gauge a woman's genuine desire.

Mother's eyes never smiled. The woman had no real emotion. Except disappointment.

They both stood up. He let the possibility that he might ask for her number linger in the air between them for about a minute. He waited until he noticed the slightest consternation in her bright green eyes.

Then...

"So can I call you?"

She smiled, and he was near positive he saw her shoulders relax. "Sure. I have a pen somewhere." She fumbled in her purse.

"I'll put it in here." He pulled out his cell phone.

"Right." She blushed.

"Full name?" He raised an eyebrow, a flirtatious glimmer in his eyes.

"Kadee Carlisle." She shot him a coy smile.

"Kadee with a D Carlisle. I like it."

She blushed, again.

She gave him her number. Then, he kissed her cheek. "I'll call you." He let his hand casually brush against hers. Their eyes locked, sending immediate electricity between them. They grinned as they parted ways.

While strolling back to his apartment, he thought about Kadee with a D. The way her hips swung when she walked, *bunk, bunk, bunk,* as they swayed side to side. *Definitely confident about her sexuality,* he thought.

Not all women were like that. In fact, lots of women concealed their sexual longings, even from themselves, in order to assert propriety. Not Kadee with a D. She seemed comfortable with herself and her sexual expression. *That* was undeniably appealing.

Yet, *that* also meant that Kadee was the kind of woman who could eat a man alive. With one effortless bat of an eyelash, a woman like Kadee with a D could ruin a man's life by enticing him with her sexual openness, then tossing him out as quickly as she reeled him in.

Mother performed such exploits countless times. Her last victim: Brock Booker Meyers. Poor guy called her constantly for more than a year after they broke up. Mother toyed with that man, made him think she seriously considered reconciliation, only to bat those mascara-thick eyelashes a few times, then say in a surgery tone: "Sorry, Brock, dear. It's over. It was never really anything serious for me. You really ought to go up a size in your pants, too. Seeing that roll of stomach fat hang over your belt was awfully unappealing, I must say."

Noah didn't hear Brock's side of the conversation. Mother dumped him over the phone. That was her usual protocol. Brock must have responded about his pants being too tight, because he heard mother say, "No, dear, it wasn't the snug pants, but those didn't help. Take care now," before she hung up the phone.

Mother's eyes glistened with a cold satisfaction when she hung up the call.

Mother crushed hearts all over Manhattan.

He would keep his guard up with Kadee.

Yvonne, on the other hand, was different. She had a pristine way about her. He knew from experience that she took love and sex seriously. Yvonne preserved sexual intimacy for relationships where there was a commitment. Sexually untarnished, she embodied the type of woman every man should marry: unspoiled, domestic, conventional.

He trusted Yvonne, too. And he never really trusted anyone. Ever since he knew her, she was the rock beside him, steady and unwavering in her support of him. Whenever he struggled with anything, Yvonne was there to help him through. Of course, he didn't tell her everything. But he did open up to her more than anyone else in his life. He loved Yvonne for that. If she could ever trust him again, he thought he would marry her.

Did he love her? Sure, he loved Yvonne. He loved her more than he loved anyone, besides father. He loved her best he could.

However, he was mildly annoyed with their current situation. He had betrayed Yvonne thirteen years ago, back when they were in medical school together. And although she was close with him as a friend, he could never win her back in any real romantic way. However, he knew with certainty that Yvonne loved him completely.

He would get her back. And he would marry her.

Last week, he had finally gotten a kiss out of her. Lord knows he had been patient. The desire built between them. He could feel it. Yet, she remained closed off to the possibility of sexual intimacy.

But he did finally get a kiss. He had only been trying for thirteen years.

Yes. She finally kissed him.

Hallelujah.

Admittedly, he had been quite the ass back in medical school. He fucked up. But everyone fucks up when their young and immature. That's what being young is for: fucking up. By the time someone is older, they will hopefully have learned a thing or two about how to live. Of course, Mother was excluded from the whole learning-from-mistakes recipe for life. Mother didn't give a rat's ass about mistakes or reparation.

He thought he had it all back then: looks, money, intelligence. Twenty six, a medical student, with lots of girls interested in hanging out with him, he didn't want to be tied to any one woman. He always had his eye on Yvonne, though. He never took his eyes off his prize. But Yvonne was not going to make it easy to win her back.

A kiss, though. That kiss last week was a step toward… something.

Yet… this Kadee intrigued him. She was different from Yvonne, sexier, more confident, unconventional. She was inconveniently captivating. And he found himself fantasizing about getting her naked for the rest of the morning. That *bunk-bunk* of her swaying hips, so graceful, so sensual, he kept imagining his hands resting along her waist as she moved them.

Noah spent the afternoon with Yvonne; the whole time he was distracted by thoughts of Kadee.

Chapter 2

2001

Noah stared at the ceiling. Yvonne nestled her naked body against his.

He wanted to make a run for it.

He shifted his position, but his discomfort continued to build. Yvonne was his friend, a good friend. He had to stay long enough to give the semblance of respectfulness.

Besides, he had tried to get Yvonne into bed since the first week he met her, her first week of medical school. He had thrown on the Donovan charm. Nothing. It took over a year. An entire year of work, real, arduous work, Yvonne did not give it up easily.

Now, finally, they had done it. He got what he wanted, and he could not get the fuck out of her apartment fast enough. What the hell was wrong with him?

He had really liked Yvonne. And how many nights had he imagined this exact scenario: having sex with her, having her naked body resting against his.

He shifted his position again.

"You OK?" she whispered in his ear.

Her hot breath weighted him down with sudden undesirable obligation.

"Fine." He tried to inconspicuously wipe her stale breath off of his skin.

He glanced at her clock hoping an hour had passed. It felt like six hours. It had only been ten minutes.

Ten minutes.

Ten torturous minutes.

The longest ten minutes of his life.

Ten minutes of lying next to her in the post coital snuggle. He had to leave — and stat. He sweated as he felt the heat of oppression tightening. He needed a shower to wash away the burden of their sex and what it meant. He needed his own bed. He needed to be alone.

"I've got to go," he said it gently. He really did like her; but being close to her after sex freaked him out. He would suffocate if he stayed.

He wanted to run as far away from her as possible.

He needed air.

She gave him sad eyes, which made him want to run even faster. *She really likes me*, he thought.

In fact, the way her eyes looked, almost pleading, freaked him out even more. *Crap, she loves me. Fuuuuuuck.*

He sat up.

"Wait. I thought you were going to stay." She reached for him.

He wiggled his body to get away from her hand. "I know. I'm sorry. I uh, just need to sleep in my own bed." He stood up.

She looked horrified and pulled the sheet all the way up to her neck to cover her otherwise naked body.

He dressed as fast as he could. He even skipped lacing up his sneakers. Tripping and getting a concussion was a small price to pay for avoiding the emotional aftermath of sex with Yvonne. He was still buttoning his shirt as he reached the front door.

"I'll call," he had mumbled right before he exited the bedroom.

She didn't get up to walk him out. *Good.* Her eyes had welled, and he thought she'd burst into tears. He did not want to have to deal with her emotions.

As far as Noah was concerned, women could be overly emotional, and he wasn't into dealing with any display of hysteria. Yvonne had always seemed independent and in control, but seeing her eyes and hearing that quiver in her voice as he departed after they had sex made him wonder if she was really a needy, annoying, overly demanding type. Mother said almost all women were like that. Mother should know. Mother was the champ at being needy.

After that night, he kept his distance from Yvonne. He didn't want her to get the wrong idea. Besides, he felt freaked out by her feelings. If she loved him, he did not want to have to deal with her. *Women in love are needy.*

Worse yet, she called a bunch of time. "Noah, at least let's talk about what happened. Did I do something wrong?"

He returned her call when he knew she was at class. "Hey, sorry we keep missing each other."

The phone tag went like that for over a week. The more she tried, the more distant he felt. He stopped returning her calls after about her fifteenth one.

Nearly two weeks after he had bolted from her bed, he was strolling home from class. His arms swung as he sang to himself. He had just aced his anatomy and physiology test — perfect score — so he was on top of the world. When he reached the front door of his apartment, he found Yvonne standing there, her foot tapping the ground. Her hair was pulled back in a tight ponytail, her blue eyes bloodshot, her skin blotchy.

Sweat broke out along his skin. "Oh. Hey." He tried to act nonchalant.

Yvonne's nostrils flared. Her eyes took on a severe look. "Have I done something to offend you? What, Noah Donovan, have I done to make you treat me with such cavalier disrespect? I'm a person. I have feelings."

"I – I – I'm sorry." He felt like a total ass, but he didn't want to deal with her. He could tell she had been crying. "I don't take your feelings for granted. I am… an ass."

"What happened meant nothing to you? Just say it. What happened meant nothing to you." Her voice was calm, but her eyes looked anguished, desperate, a little angry.

He felt defensive, but tried to remain diplomatic. He didn't want her to freak out on him. "It did mean something. But I don't want a relationship. I thought I made that clear. We're friends. Right?"

Her eyes shot open. The blue of her irises became huge. "No. You did not make that clear. I take sexual intimacy very seriously, Noah Donovan. I am not some pawn to be toyed with emotionally. I would never have given myself to you if I thought for one itsy-bitsy second you intended to be friends with benefits. I don't do that." Those baby blues of hers shot daggers at him as her nostrils flared. "So, friends? No. We're not friends. Don't call me again." She stormed away.

Good. I won't. He puffed out a long sigh of relief, as he watched her go.

The relief lasted for a couple of months. But he started to miss her.

Worse yet, she blew him off a few times at parties when he tried to ask how she was doing.

She wasn't mean or nasty. He wished she was. It would have shown that she still gave a shit about him. Instead, she smiled coldly, said nothing, then walked away.

It made him nuts. He wanted her to talk to him.

So after some contemplation, he called her to apologize, to revisit the whole mistake-having-sex situation. Maybe he made a mistake. Part of him wanted her again. The first few times she didn't pick up. Finally, on his fifth attempt, she answered.

"I thought I asked you not to call me." She said, a self-righteous pinch in her tone.

"Yvonne. Listen. I made a mistake. I'm sorry. Please can we talk about it?"

"There is nothing to talk about. You are a jerk. And that's the truth."

"Yes. A big jerk. Please. Let's grab a drink and discuss my jerkiness."

"Cute. But no. I'm not into replays."

"I miss our friendship. Let me take you to dinner."

"No."

"Please. I really am sorry. Please." The line went silent. He could not even hear her breathing. "Yvonne? You still there?"

"Fine, you can buy me a very expensive dinner. But do not even think about touching me. Got it?"

"Yes. Got it."

It didn't take long for them to gain their friendship rhythm back. A few months after, their comfort level now reestablished, he had a burning desire to have sex with her again. In fact, he leaned in for a kiss one night while they were out drinking at a local bar. A brazen move. Yvonne flashed him a stern look as she pushed him away. "You must be nuts if you think I'd ever hooked up with you again. You're lucky I'm even your friend after what you did to me."

"Sorry. You're right." He said. But in the back of his mind he constantly tried to figure out how to reel her in again. He could tell that she still had romantic interest; she probably even loved him.

But Yvonne was a tough cookie. When she made her mind up, she stuck to her guns. And Noah was never able to get back what he had lost when he emotionally abandoned her that morning. Eventually, he gave up on the sexual relationship and instead developed a very close friendship with her.

Over time, Noah's sexual curiosities and attraction for Yvonne developed into authentic feelings. Noah wasn't sure what to do with them or even exactly what they were. One night while they sat shoulder to shoulder at a bar, he concluded that he loved Yvonne.

He had fallen in love with Yvonne.

It must be love, he had said to himself. *I think about her all the time.*

But Yvonne was steadfast; he couldn't even get a kiss on the lips from her.

His chance was gone.

Four years after their sexual encounter, Yvonne married another man: Dustin Stone, also a doctor. Noah acted happy for them, a part of him was. The other part of him waited for the day Yvonne would come to her senses and give him another chance.

He felt like a total dick. He was waiting to steal a woman from another man. Well, not steal, really. More like take Dustin's sloppy seconds. But in reality, Yvonne was no sloppy second. She was his first choice. And he might not have to wait too long. She had disclosed to Noah on a few occasions that she wasn't sure she had made the right decision marrying Dustin.

In fact, Yvonne's complaints about Dustin reminded him a lot of the times when Mother would complain to him about his father. Ironically, his father and Dustin were both surgeons. Both worked insane hours at the hospital.

Mother used to come into his bedroom on the nights his father stayed at the hospital and crawl into bed with him. She grabbed him so close, sometimes he felt suffocated. She'd say things like, "Thank goodness Mother has you to love her. A woman needs love from a man, and your father has none to give."

One night when he was only six years old, his mother crawled in next to him. "I know someday you will leave me. Just please don't leave me now. Mother needs you. And always remember, no woman will ever love you the way Mother does."

She scrunched up against him so tight, he could feel her breasts caressing his back, and he realized she was naked.

He felt a strange physical sensation lying there with her, a good sensation, excited, aroused, but also ashamed. His eyes remained wide open, a confused terror in his gaze. Mother's breath blew warm against his back, and he wanted to escape her grasp. Her ever-tightening embrace. Her suffocating clutches. It felt like she clutched him. Once he knew she had fallen asleep, he moved away from her, all the way to the edge of the bed. He scrunched his pillow in front of him and buried his head in it.

When he woke up in the morning, her bare body was wrapped around him again.

Chapter 3

PRESENT DAY

Dinner with Kadee with a D didn't have to be a big deal. A secret and a lie weren't the same thing.

I have as much right to my privacy as anyone else. Besides, Yvonne is only a friend. Since I have no obligation to tell her anything, it isn't really a secret.

Noah rushed home from his date with Yvonne to call Kadee to ask her to dinner.

When he had mentioned to Yvonne that he wasn't feeling well and needed to leave their museum excursion prematurely, she looked irritated. But she didn't share any annoyance, instead she had said, "Oh, that's too bad. Can I do anything?"

Yvonne rarely demonstrated her feelings, but her nostrils always gave her away. They would flare just a little when she was upset. Or a lot, depending on the severity of her ire.

"No. It's OK. A migraine is all. I need to go home and sleep it off."

The lie made it a secret. Lying to women came as naturally as brushing his teeth. It was a survival mechanism Noah had learned from his early life, a way to maintain some autonomy from Mother. Benign little lies weren't deceitful. They were merely a way to maintain some freedom.

Nooooo big deal.

This little Kadee secret certainly was nothing compared to the secret Mother had.

Yvonne's nostrils expanded. "OK. I see. Migraines are awful. Let's go then."

He wrapped his arm around her shoulders; they headed out of the museum. During the entire walk home with Yvonne, he thought of what he would say to Kadee.

When they arrived in front of Yvonne's apartment, he kissed her cheek, said, "Love you."

She pursed her lips, blinked a few times. He felt certain it was code for "me too, but I'm not going to say it back."

I'll come by your office for lunch Monday, or do you want to have dinner tomorrow if I'm feeling better?"

"Let's make it lunch on Monday. Ta, ta, handsome."

"Monday, then." He smiled. He loved when she called him handsome.

Yvonne was easy. People who trusted were always easy. Getting rid of his obligation for dinner with Mother would be a different story. Mother trusted nothing and no one. Lucky for Noah, he had learned to navigate his way around Mother. The only way to maintain a relationship with doting, suffocating Mother was to become as artful at deceit as she was.

"Mother, I can't go to dinner tonight. I'm not feeling well. I'm sorry."

"Mother will come over and take care of you."

"No. Please, Mother. It's a migraine. I need to sleep it off." He rolled his eyes.

"It's Yvonne. She's given you a headache. She talks too much."

No, you do, he thought. "I'll call you in the morning when I feel better. Sorry about tonight."

"Did you call Lillian?"

Homely Lillian Seasons. "No. I'll call her first thing tomorrow. I promise."

"First thing. She's waiting."

"OK. I will. Love you. Bye."

"Bye-bye."

He took a heavy breath. Getting out of an obligation with Mother was not a small feat. This susceptibility he had to getting migraines turned out to be one of his greatest allies against Mother.

Hallelujah.

A mix of convoluted thoughts swarmed around his mind as he strolled over to the restaurant to meet Kadee. He had been so focused on the get-Kadee-to-dinner mission, he hadn't given much thought beyond her, "I'd love to grab dinner tonight," response.

What was he doing? Yvonne seemed to be coming around. Now he was off to have dinner with another woman, a sensuous woman. Those green eyes and *bunk-bunk* hips distracted him all day at the museum. And that carefree way about her meant the woman was an emotional danger zone.

If provocative women were forced to wear STOP signs, which honestly they should be, Kadee would have a huge blinking sign, maybe even one that was lit up with red neon lights. The woman could not be trusted. And yet, here he was, Dr. Noah Donovan, son of Dangling Donovan — as the gossiping neighbors had called his mother during her hospital stay — strutting over to meet an untrustworthy woman.

Kadee reminded him a lot of the girls he always liked in high school and college, the ones who never even gave him a second look because he was tall and awkward, the smart, non-athletic, two-left-feet-type. Girls weren't into him back then, at least not the prettiest girls. The only time they paid him any mind was when they needed help with their science or math homework.

But he was a doctor now, and he had matured into his striking looks. And as Mother repeatedly reminded him: "Women always want a handsome doctor. You must be very, very selective."

And mother was right. He had many more opportunities with women as a grown man. It wasn't being a doctor, though; it had more to do with the confidence. Women enjoyed a strong, self-assured man. Once he realized that that was what women wanted, he became a master at exuding it.

The Donovan charm, as he called it. He noticed his charisma as early as medical school. It had become increasingly refined over the years, and the greater the charm, the more attention he would get.

But this new attention he received also meant that he needed to be highly cautious of women, especially the ones who wouldn't have been interested in him prior to developing his appeal: women exactly like Kadee. In fact, as an endeavor to condition his ability to read women, he had spent quite a bit of time with paid escorts. He'd hire them to ask all kinds of questions about the female gender. Pay enough money and people will dish out just about anything, including information. The wild sex was an added bonus.

April, one of the whores, was known for giving showers: a cute little name to go with her not-so-cute specialty. He wasn't particularly into golden showers. He liked taking them alone and without the "golden." The shower was a private haven for him. But he did enjoy April's company. She had thick blonde hair down to her waist and enormous breasts. He enjoyed making her wince by yanking her hair as he thrust into her. She took it hard and, for an extra hundred, up the ass.

April had told him that some women marry for love and others for money. No big stunning insight. But she also had told him what to look for. "Beautiful women," she had told him one day in her raspy voice, "know how to use their beauty to get things. Sexy women, know how to use their sexuality to get things. Sexually open women can be the most dangerous. Not all, but some.

"It's a fallacy that men control the world. Women's sexuality controls everything. Everything. Marquis de Sade wrote about the power of women's sexuality, and he was locked up for it. No one wants to admit it, but it is the truth. I know firsthand," she motioned to her naked body, "just how much a woman can get and how far a woman can go if she is willing to use her body."

She then added, "You're a hotty, Doctah D. What woman wouldn't want to scoop you up? Just be smart about it. Use your noggin, if you know what I mean." She giggled. "Everyone shows their true colors if you give them enough time. Never let yourself jump in too fast. Make her prove her love before you trust her, and you'll be fine."

April was his favorite little whore.

She offered a plethora of eye-opening information. It made him understand Mother better, too. And that was not a small thing. Understanding Mother was like cracking the Rubik's cube. Not easy. For some, impossible. But once someone did it, it was easier to conquer the next time. Mother ensnared his father, a handsome, wealthy Bostonian surgeon. She probably studied de Sade like the Bible.

So, the impossibly alluring Kadee with a D could not be trusted. But he had to get to know her at least a little. Maybe a nice casual fling, if he could break through that armor she seemed to have. A few exciting nights out on the town with wild, subversive Kadee with a D.

Noooo, big deal.

Nothing serious.

It didn't have to interfere with his relationship with Yvonne. Besides, there was nothing between them — yet — beyond friendship. They kissed once in her office. Not a big deal. A small deal, actually. Yvonne put the brakes on before it even got heated. She kissed him like they were in the fifth grade and sharing their first-ever kiss. Just a little tongue, then she put a stop to it. "I'm sorry. I'm not ready to go any further, handsome." She flashed him those baby blues.

He had responded. *"OK. I understand."*

But he didn't really understand. Enough was enough. He had paid for his mistake.

Maybe Kadee was exactly what he needed while he waited for Yvonne to come around.

Kadee stood in front of the restaurant waiting as he walked up. Striking was an understatement. Kadee looked like a model. Her dark hair, thick and straight, hung down to the middle of her back. He noticed the slight tousle. Immediately, he imagined pulling on it while he planted a hard kiss on her mouth.

Suave was an understatement when it came to Noah's uncanny ability to interest the opposite sex. But, he swallowed hard when he saw Kadee, as he wondered if he could rouse her interest. Would Kadee with a D fall for the Donovan charm?

"You're a hotty, Doctah. D. What woman wouldn't want to scoop you up?" Nothing as honest as a whore, he smiled as he recalled April's wisdoms. *You got this, Donovan.*

"Hi," he smiled. "You look stunning."

"Hi," she smiled back. "You too." She chuckled. Although she had a proud strength about her, she also had a casual, easy-going manner. Kadee with a D seemed complicated.

"Shall we?"

"Sure."

The hostess took them to their table. A little hole-in-the-wall Italian place, the sweet aroma of tomato sauce immediately filled Noah's nostrils. The tables on either side of them were occupied. Kadee and Noah had to squeeze into their spot. Once they sat and he looked at her bright green eyes across the table, he didn't even notice the other restaurant occupants. Kadee's eyes possessed a concentrated, inquisitive look, like she hung on his every word. He enjoyed seeing that expression in them. But he wanted to know more about her.

"So tell me what interested you in the criminal mind? I'm intrigued." He placed his hand over hers as she talked.

He saw the slightest blush of her cheeks.

"I have always been interested in the darker aspects of human nature and personality."

"Me too. I went into medicine almost like it was what I was supposed to do, but I like psychology, too. I took a few classes in college. What made you apply for your doctorate?"

"I studied psychology and criminology in college. I got a masters degree from John Jay a while back. I thought I'd go into law enforcement, actually. But then I landed a research job for the city. I was working on a research grant about crime in the inner city. Then when the grant ended, I applied for my doctorate. I'm researching passionate homicide."

He smiled. "People who kill their lovers?"

"Something like that. How love turns to murder, essentially. But I'm interested in psychology in general, too. What makes people do what they do. Nothing is more interesting than that."

His eyes glistened. "I agree. People are full of surprises. So how *does* love turn to murder?"

"Ah. That's a complicated question. All human behaviors are complex and filled with individual variability. But I can say that love and passion, just like all human emotion, are filled with paradox and contradiction. Passion is an emotion that draws people together. It's also one that drives people apart. Love and hate are basically two sides of the same coin. Murder happens when the hate turns to rage and the person loses control."

He made a steeple with his hands, rested his chin on the top as he contemplated. "What if love isn't love, but need? What if the love only looked like love while underneath it was really a desperate yearning for someone — or anyone. Then the killing would look like love turned homicidal, but really it was an act of desperation."

"Hmm... interesting twist." She paused. He could see her mulling over the idea. "Like I said, there are no definitives. So yes, I believe this is one possibility. But I also would argue that when love turns to murder, there is always some desperation. That's what I love about psychology. There never ceases to be new ways to think about human behavior or new ideas to develop. If we still know each other when I finish my dissertation, I'll let you read it if you want." She chuckled.

He squeezed her hand across the table. "You are an interesting woman. And smart. I like that."

She blushed. "Thanks."

"You probably hear this all the time. You are very beautiful."

Their eyes met. "Thank you."

They held eye contact. Noah reached for his wine, sipped while keeping his gaze locked to hers.

This woman had him mesmerized. Sure, she was stunning, but it wasn't simply how she looked, something stirred underneath. An edge, waywardness, something unconventional, something complicated, like she had layers upon layers to her. People were often one-dimensional. That was a good thing because it made most people easy to understand, but this Kadee, she had something intriguing about her. And he wanted to know more.

Yet, he was assured that Kadee was the type of woman who used her sexuality to control men. The woman had a blaring STOP sign on her chest. Actually, Kadee's sign said: STOP *and* BEWARE. If he was going to be intimate with her, he had to keep his guard up. Keep it light and casual. Otherwise, she might demolish him.

Later as he walked Kadee to her apartment, he endured an unusual inner dialogue. He wanted to ask her for a nightcap. Maybe get her to invite him. But he also felt reticent. It was his desire. He wanted to rip her clothes off. The idea of seeing Kadee and her *bunk-bunk* hips naked preoccupied him. A restlessness enveloped him. But he could not act on emotion. He needed to dictate his decisions about Kadee with rationality only. He needed to remain in control of himself — and of her. If he was going to be fucking around with Kadee, it had to be on his terms.

"You wanna come up? I have a nice bottle of red?" He could hear the hesitancy in her voice when she asked, almost like she was afraid of his response. *Good,* he thought.

He took both her hands in his, gazed into her eye, said nothing. The pull to kiss her was strong, but he was stronger. She looked at him, her piercing green eyes filled with desire for him. And it felt so good, like he was on top of the world. What man wouldn't want to feel like that. God, he wanted to fuck her. Right then. ON the street. Let go. Lose control. But… he had to hold back.

He kissed her on the lips. They felt soft. *I could get lost in those lips.* He wanted to go further. Much further. He restrained his impulses. "Not tonight, Kadee, but thank you." She looked surprised that he turned her down. He loved seeing her confused expression. He was sure she doubted herself, wondering if there was something wrong with her.

Of course, she was surprised.

Kadee probably controlled every man she came into contact with.

*Not anymore, Ka**dee**.*

"I had a nice time with you, Kadee with a D." He winked, said, "I'll call you."

She gave an apprehensive smile. "Um… OK. Sounds good."

As he walked away, he wanted to turn back to see if she was watching him. He could feel her eyes glued to his back, but he didn't know if it was intuition or simply a wish. He made himself continue on and decided, without looking back, that she was watching him.

He'd call her tomorrow, for sure.

Chapter 4

Noah arrived home around midnight from his date with Kadee. Mother had left three voice mails, two on his cell, one on his landline. Not unusual and nothing important. *"Checking in to see how you're feeling, dear. You must be sleeping."* The calls weren't genuine concern, rather a ruse to interfere with his life. He rolled his eyes. The woman would stop at nothing to know every minute detail of his life.

He had tried to set boundaries: "Mother, I'm a grown man now. I need space and privacy."

"Mother is giving you your privacy, dear. I bought you your own apartment. All we have is each other. It's been very hard for Mother, raising you all alone since your father passed. I do the best I can to make sure you have everything you need. To provide you with the luxuries that I didn't have as a younger person. Do you not appreciate all that I have done for you?"

"I do. Of course, I do."

Negotiating with Mother was like trying to tame a tiger in the wild, impossible to do without getting eaten alive.

Besides, Mother *had* raised him all alone. There was no denying what she had sacrificed for him. There were men after father passed away, but none whom she remained attached to. She insisted it was because she didn't want anyone to come between them. "We must never let anyone or anything come between us," she would say. When he was a boy this pleased him, but as a man it emasculated him. He was her son, her husband, her confidante, her doctor, her… everything.

Clearly, the woman had an insatiable need for him. And most times, he felt smothered. "No one will ever love you like Mother," she always said. She repeated it so often, it practically left tread marks on her tongue. Mother's love was so powerful, it strangled him.

Mother didn't like Yvonne, either. He worried how it would all go to go down if Yvonne ever agreed to give him a second chance. He could predict what Mother would say: "She's too old; she's too fat; she's too mousy." As though Lillian Seasons wasn't mousy? Lillian was the epitome of mousy.

He hopped in the shower, put the water as hot as he could take it without scalding himself and let the water trickle over his body.

Thirty minutes later, he lay in bed, the comforter lazily draped across half his body. He thought of Kadee. He'd call her tomorrow, but not until late in the day. Maybe ask her to dinner on Tuesday night. He didn't even know exactly what he wanted from her. All he knew was he wanted something. That carefree way about her, that waywardness, he enjoyed that about her. He could tell she was strong, too. Strong and sexy, and he wondered for a moment if it was a mistake to even get involved with her, even casually.

"You'll keep it under control, Donovan," he reassured himself, then rolled over and fell asleep.

Noah and Belle sitting in a tree K-I-S-S-I-N-G. First comes love, then comes the berry, then comes daddy in the cemetery.

Noah sat straight up in bed, his eyes filled with a harrowing fear. The sing-song rhythm wouldn't stop. He put his hands over his ears, shook his head, tried to get the kids' voices to quiet. He hated when he had that dream, a memory, really. It had been a few years since he had it. But there it was, the eerie harmony of voices from his childhood. The kids teasing him right after his father had died. Mother had to be hospitalized, and he stayed with the neighbors. It was just about the worst thing a ten-year-old kid could go through. Losing one parent, suddenly, and having the other stricken with an "illness" immediately following.

Noah and Belle sitting in a tree K-I-S-S-I-N-G. First comes love, then comes the berry...

He hurried to his iPod station and put on music. He did not care what it was, just as long as it had lyrics. He needed something with words to drown out the memory of that haunting rhyme.

The next morning, Mother called: 9:30 a.m., right on the nose. Not one minute before or after 9:30 a.m. Mother's punctuality was incessant. Noah groaned as he rolled over. As if her call wasn't annoying enough, his head was pounding. He lost so much sleep due to that damn dream. The music had done nothing to help. Finally at 7 a.m., he had fallen back to sleep from sheer exhaustion, but the stress of the memory gave him a migraine.

Serves me right, he thought. He had lied to Mother, said he had a migraine. Now, he actually did have one. The woman even had power over his headaches. He didn't want to talk. But if he didn't pick up, she would keep calling until he did, the *brrrring* of the phone pounding against his aching temples and forehead like a sledgehammer. He sheltered his eyes from the painful light with one hand, and with the other he picked up the phone. "Good morning, Mother."

"How are you feeling, dear? Better I hope. You slept for a long while last night."

Her tone had a bite. He wondered if she knew he had gone out.

"Actually, I've still got the headache." He eased out of bed and shuffled to the bathroom, still shading his eyes from the morning sun blinding him through the windows.

He opened the medicine cabinet. Popped a migraine pill.

"It's Yvonne." His mother's judgmental voice pierced his ears like ice picks. "She's the type of woman who could give any man a headache. Droning on and on about nothing. And on and on and on and — ".

"Please. My head. Please. Can we talk a little later?"

"Fine. I'm going to brunch with Paul Shapiro. I'll stop by afterward. I'll bring you some eggs."

Paul Shapiro: her lawyer, occasional sex partner and innocent victim of Mother's exquisite chicanery. Mother kept the poor guy on a leash just loose enough to maintain the illusion that his decisions were his own, which came in handy when she needed company at dinner, company in bed or his lawyerly expertise. "No. That's OK. I need to sleep. I'll call you later. Have a nice time."

"Love you, dear."

"Love you."

He released a sigh, flopped back into bed and slept until 2 p.m. When he finally woke up, the afternoon sun warming his bedroom, his headache was gone.

Mother had left a message while he slept, which both annoyed him and relieved him. Mother could do that to a person: make someone feel such a complex mix of emotions that even the most imperturbable individual would be cast into thane abyss of emotional chaos.

Lillian Seasons. Mother had called Lillian Seasons — mousy, homely Lillian Seasons — to tell her that Noah had a headache and would be calling to invite her out to dinner when he felt better. He was forty years old. Fucking forty and Mother had called to schedule his date. Not even the date. She scheduled the future invitation to a date. His headache might be gone, but now he needed a massage to alleviate the stress tension in his neck and shoulders.

The good news: Lillian Seasons reunited with her ex-boyfriend, a doctor who worked in the morgue. *Perfect,* he thought. Mother's last comment: *"Poor girl. Her loss."*

Her loss, my gain, Mother.

Theo, his buddy from medical school, had also called asking to meet up for a burger and a beer. Noah called Theo back, made a plan to meet him that evening. Then he called Mother; thankfully, she had a fund-raiser event and couldn't talk.

Thank God for the little things. As he went to the kitchen to get a glass of cold water, those haunting voices started again: *Noah and Belle sitting in a tree K-I-S-S-I-N-G. First comes love...*

Ugh! He rubbed the front of his head. Why was that song playing in his mind all of sudden? He put music on: Metallica's "Nothing Else Matters" blasted out of the speakers.

Chapter 5

Sunday evening, 9:00 p.m., and he arrived home after hanging out with Theo. A couple beers, a burger and the football game made for a relaxing evening uncomplicated by the female gender. A short guy with broad shoulders and a crooked smile, Theo had been married for five years. His wife, Natalie, a brunette with small dark eyes, thin lips and no ass, let Theo out of his cage on Sundays to watch the game.

Theo repeatedly gave Noah shit for bouncing from one woman to the next without making any real commitment. "You're the stereotype of the over-forty, never-been-married New York guy. Natalie says you're a walking red flag."

"Thank Natalie for the compliment." Noah gave an acerbic laugh. *Yeah, thank Natalie and her flat ass.* "I'm enjoying myself. Nothing wrong with that. I like my freedom."

"I hear you." Theo patted his shoulder.

Yvonne had texted while he was out: *Can you come for lunch tomorrow at 1:00, instead of 12:30?*

Yvonne often changed their plans by the half hour. A weird little quirk of hers. He chuckled at the text message. He found her predictability comforting.

His response: *Sure, no prob. See you then.*

☺ *Thanks handsome.* She fired right back.

A smile crossed his face as he thought about Yvonne. Yvonne was probably the only person in his adult life that he ever really trusted. Sure, he trusted Theo and a couple of his other buddies, but not like Yvonne. Sometimes he told her things that he never even dreamed he would say out loud. Like his conflicts with Mother, his fear of dying from some awful illness, even about being bullied as a kid. He was so ashamed about that, but one day he found himself telling her without reservation.

She had said, "Oh, handsome, kids can be so mean. They were probably just jealous of you. Kids tease the kids who are different, and different kids are often the ones who grow up to be the most revered. Like you." She batted her eyelashes at him and gave him that warm signature smile of hers filled with genuine love and admiration.

She always made him feel so good.

He even told her the truth about the fight between Mother and his father. It spilled out of his mouth unexpectedly. Her jaw dropped. She rubbed his shoulder. "It's OK, handsome. You didn't do anything wrong."

"Didn't I?" he had said.

"It's not your fault." She smiled lovingly, took his hand in hers.

"Let's change the subject."

And she did. She never brought it up again, either. Although a few times he could tell she wanted to.

When he thought about Yvonne, really thought about her, he thought maybe he shouldn't pursue this whole Kadee-thing. But, Yvonne was only a friend. A relationship with her was nothing more than a hopeful possibility. At least that's what he convinced himself as he reached for his phone to call Kadee.

Not really in the mood for a get-to-know-you-better chat, he decided to text Kadee instead of calling: *Had a great time last night. Dinner Tuesday?*

Some things shouldn't be done so cavalierly. Some things can't be reversed once put into motion. And sometimes, something seemingly innocent can be duly nefarious, leading down a dark path of self-destruction.

Chapter 6

Tuesday afternoon at the office. In between his patient appointments, Noah was distracted by thoughts of Kadee. This was unusual because Noah was an exceptional compartmentalizer. Most doctors were. Having to be present for patients made the ability to shove personal issues onto the back burner a vital technique. Yet, Kadee's green eyes, those *bunk-bunk* hips, the intense sexuality she exuded, all preoccupied him. He felt positive they would be intimate later. That excited him.

She had texted back: *I had a great time, too. Tuesday night's good. I'm free after 6.*

A jolt of exhilaration coursed through him when he received her response. He had to admit he was eager to see Kadee with a D.

Later, while he got ready to meet her, he reminded himself to be wary of her, to not under any circumstance, let this woman get under his skin or close to his heart. But when he arrived at the restaurant and saw her, that plan flew out the window.

"Come on, tell me about you. I'm sick of talking about me." Her eyes had that penetrating, concentrated gaze; her intensity almost felt magnetic, pulling him toward her, even though he tried to resist. Next thing he knew, his hand was on her leg; he rubbed her thigh, not a contrived gesture, but true desire to touch her.

He wanted her.

God, did he want her.

An hour later they were back at his apartment. Her clothes were off almost as soon as he closed his front door. Kadee was naked, and just about the most gorgeous woman he had even seen. Certainly the most gorgeous one he had ever had back to his apartment. Her hips were so round. His hands fit perfectly on them as he pulled her close.

It wasn't just her physicality, though. Her eyes and her lips, her countenance as he touched her all over, kissed her neck, read the pleasure on her face and in her body language. That felt amazing. Watching her respond to him, made him feel on top of the world, strong, masculine, confident.

He was *the man*. He was a fucking god!

Later as they lay in his bed, he noticed a peaceful smile on her lips as she relaxed against him. He ran his fingers through her thick hair. *You've got this, Donovan.* He watched her sleep for a while before dozing off himself.

Noah woke up early the next morning and looked at Kadee sleeping next to him, so stunning and naked and vulnerable.

He kissed her neck until she stirred awake. She turned, grabbed him tight. Her skin felt soft against his. He wanted her again, badly. Noah never liked morning sex. He always felt like he needed a shower first, but the pull to be intimate with Kadee overpowered the need to wash himself. In fact, Noah could not remember ever feeling so sexually drawn to a woman before.

Passion filled the apartment that morning. So enraptured with Kadee, he even let an early-morning call from Mother go to voice mail. She called his cell after the landline. The *brrrring* of Mother's calls made it feel like she stood over them in his apartment. Mother invaded him and their privacy. He shut off both of his phones so they could enjoy each other without Mother's intrusion.

He made Kadee a quick breakfast. He had to leave by 10 a.m. to make his patient appointments. Before he said anything about departing, Kadee said, "I have to go. I'm meeting my friend for yoga."

He felt an unexpected burning in his heart. Her saying she had to leave before he had the chance to say the same made him uncomfortable. Was she done with him already? He responded, "I have to go, too. Morning patients."

She smiled at him, exposing her affection. She exuded a warmth, but the erectness of her posture, her shoulders back in a proud stance and that slight pucker of her lips betrayed her self-possessed, flirtatious nature. Kadee's beauty and confidence, that wall she still maintained around her, intimidated Noah. Yet, those same qualities aroused him.

Noah kept himself under tight emotional control. He responded to people and situations with his intellect, but this thing that Kadee radiated had him saying, "I had such a nice time, Kadee with a D. When can we do this again? Are you free Friday night?" It slipped by his lips and into the space between them before he could stop the words, leaving him feeling vulnerable. He hated feeling exposed, which made him cringe. He hoped she didn't notice. He wanted to pull the words back before she could say she wasn't available, playing those games that women like Kadee always played.

But then those flirty eyes morphed into the glow of genuine admiration, almost the same look Yvonne had when she gazed up at him lovingly. "Yes, I'd like that. Friday night is great."

Maybe he was wrong about Kadee. Maybe she was safe. With that, Noah pulled her close, "Just one more kiss."

She wrapped her arms around him, pulled him against her. It felt great having Kadee pressed against him. Too great. Irresistibly great.

He called Mother on the way to the office, told her that his headache had come back, so he had shut off his phone. If he continued to see Kadee, which he thought he would, he'd have to tell Mother before she found out on her own — which Mother would. The woman knew everything. She never ceased to flummox him with her knack for invading his privacy.

"Are you drinking enough water, dear?"

"Yes, of course."

"Well. I think you should have blood taken. Maybe there's something wrong. It's abnormal to have a headache for four days in a row."

"I'm fine, Mother."

"Doctor's make the worst patients. You never listen."

"I always listen."

"You don't take good care of yourself. You stay up too late. You don't eat enough. Do I need to have groceries shipped to your apartment again?"

"I'm fine." Now he really did have a headache again. Clearly mother held a superior talent for making his head pound. "I'll have someone at the office take blood. OK?"

"Yes, dear. Good. I'm still going to have some groceries shipped to you. If I don't take care of you, I really worry about your health."

"I've got to go. I'll talk to you later."

"Food will be there later today. Love you, dear."

"Love you."

He pushed the call end button hard. He wanted to fling the phone, smash it against the brick wall of the Upper Eastside townhouse he was walking by. The one owned by that wealthy, stuck-up friend of Mother's.

Sometimes he hated her.

The morning flew by. Noah, busy with patients, hadn't had time to think about Kadee. But when he put his windbreaker on to go to Yvonne's office for their Monday lunch, he could smell the dullest scent of Kadee on it. He thought of her naked body nestled up next to him. A lump of desire sat in his throat.

He wanted to text her. *No man, do not text her.*

"Hi handsome," Yvonne's blue eyes sparkled as soon as he entered her office.

Did he feel guilty for sleeping with Kadee?

No. He did not.

Yvonne was only his friend. He had been trying to win Yvonne back for thirteen years, and still the woman would not budge. Besides, he hated guilt. A wasted emotion, he tried to tell himself, yet one that haunted him ever since he was a boy and he overheard his parents arguing about him.

His father's death was his fault.

Yvonne had made them egg salad sandwiches with celery pieces mixed in: his favorite.

They sat at her desk, a long cherrywood, antique, their two chairs nestled side by side.

Yvonne's shoulder brushed up against his, which felt nice.

"You look tired. Rough night?" She asked between chews.

"I'm fine."

She gave him a curious look. "You don't look fine. In fact, you have those bags under your eyes that you get when your mother's stressing you out. Something happen?"

"No. Mother's Mother. She's always driving me nuts. I'm used to it. I just didn't sleep well."

She rubbed his thigh. "Oh. That's too bad. You know those new yoga classes have really been helping me with my stress levels. I sleep better, too."

Noah felt a rush of heat. "Where did you say that yoga class was?"

Would be just his luck if Kadee and Yvonne took the same class.

"New York Sports Club on seventy-sixth. Same gym I've been going to for the last three years."

"Oh. Right."

He'd have to find out where Kadee's class was.

"You want to come with me?"

"Maybe. Sometime."

The Upper Eastside was not that big. Shit.

"You want some tea?" Yvonne got up. "I've got that orange flavor we both enjoy."

"Sure."

Yvonne filled two mugs from her electric kettle. Noah moved over to her couch, stretched his long legs.

The cups steamed as Yvonne brought them over. She sat next to him, which was unusual. She usually sat across from him in the chair. Today she sat right next to him, her thigh rubbing up against his.

She gave him big doe-eyes, too. She never did that. In that moment, he realized that Yvonne hoped he would kiss her. She pursed her lips, then licked them.

He had tried to kiss her again after that first kiss a couple weeks before. Yvonne only allowed a lip kiss, no tongue. She stopped him with, "I'm sorry. I'm not ready to go further."

"Will you ever be ready?" He had asked impatiently.

"I– I don't know. I hope so. I'm sorry. I'm still healing from my divorce. I need you as a friend right now. Maybe in time."

He had backed off.

But she seemed different now. Maybe she had had a change of heart. Yvonne was not the type to make the first move, so perhaps this was the green light so *he* could initiate. Those sky-blue eyes, huge and wanting, said, *You can kiss me now, handsome; I'm ready.*

When it rains, it pours, he thought. He hit the hottest piece of ass he had ever experienced last night. And he actually thought he liked Kadee, maybe as more than just a purely sexual plaything. Now, the woman he had been waiting for, the woman he loved, wanted him.

"Are you sure you're OK?" Yvonne looked at him, a concerned expression on her face.

She loves me, he thought. *Yvonne loves me.*

"I'm perfect." He put his hands on her cheeks, turned her face, placed a soft kiss on her lips. The faint flavor of orange tea filled his mouth when he slipped his tongue into hers. He pulled her close to him. They kissed and embraced for the next thirty minutes.

Leaving Yvonne's office that day, Noah tried to tell himself that he would see where it went with Yvonne while he let this thing, whatever it was, play out with Kadee.

No big deal.

People did this all the time.

Life was all about experiences.

He'd live in the moment.

Chapter 7

Noah and Belle sitting in a tree K-I-S-S-I-N-G. First comes love, then comes the berry, then comes daddy in the cemetery.

Noah sat up, put his hand across his chest, gasped for air.

"You alright?" Kadee looked over from her side of the bed. Half asleep with one eye still closed, she put her hand on his back.

Middle of January. The wind howled against Noah's bedroom windows. The room was dark. He glanced over at Kadee; her body looked like a shadow in the darkness.

"Bad dream?" she whispered.

"Uh, huh," he responded almost inaudibly.

She pulled him next to her, spooned him. "You wanna tell me about it?"

"No. That's alright. I have this thing. Never talk about your bad dreams. It makes them seem more real."

"It's the opposite. Talk about your bad dreams to release whatever thoughts and feelings have led to them."

Yvonne had told him the same thing.

"You sound like a shrink."

"Come on. Don't deflect what I said. I want to know more about you. We've been together for three months, and I don't feel like I know much about you at all."

"Not now. It's four a.m."

"Alright. Alright. You are a mystery man." She kissed his back. "My mystery man."

"Here. Hold me tight" He pulled her long arms around his chest, held her hands in front of his face.

He fell back into a restless sleep and a scene from his childhood played in his mind.

"Thank you, Mother."

Belle tapped her cheek, motioning Noah to give her a kiss.

"It's my favorite color, too. Blue." He leaned over and kissed Mother's cheek.

His tenth birthday. The last birthday he would spend with his father.

His parents had bought him the bicycle he had wanted.

The scene shifted. It was later that same day when he overheard his father adamantly telling Mother he was leaving and taking Noah with him.

Noah lay in his bed. His bedroom door cracked open, a thin line of light shining in the otherwise dark room. He squeezed his pillow as tight as he could, frightened.

His father had a formidable voice; it bellowed easily into Noah's bedroom. "You touched him inappropriately. More than once, Belle. I'm taking him away from you before it's too late."

"I did nothing of the sort. You're never home. I sleep with Noah. It's a way for us to deal with your constant absence from the family."

Annabel. I walked in on you holding our son's hand on your naked breast."

"Nonsense. We were sleeping. It was an innocent accident."

"It's not the first time you've done something inappropriate. I caught you sleeping naked next to him two nights ago when I came home late. I'm certain this has been going on for a while. It makes me sick. I can't believe I didn't realize it sooner. I've seen the way you look at him. You kiss him like a lover." He took a calming breath and tempered his voice. "I've spoken with a colleague of mine. If you give up all parental rights, I won't press changes. Otherwise, I will make sure you are held legally accountable for your actions. And you will lose custody, anyway. I am doing this to protect Noah. Listen to what I am saying, Annabel."

"I've done nothing wrong. I'm not giving up my Noah. He's my whole life."

Noah sobbed softly into his pillow. His father came to the door, "It's OK, son."

He went to Noah, pulled the covers over him, kissed his cheek and closed the door.

The scene shifted again: his father on the floor in the kitchen grabbing his chest, groaning, Mother hovering over him.

"What happened?" Noah cried. Terror washed over him.

Mother's eyes darted around, in a stern voice she said, "Go back to your room, dear."

Noah ran back to his room, horrified. Tears gushed out of his eyes. He grabbed his pillow, put it in front of his chest, punched it over and over. If his father was hurt, it was his fault.

Sirens blasted and a group of people came into their house. Mother locked him in his bedroom, but he heard hurried, pressured voices, Mother screaming, "Do something, do something. Please help my husband."

He cried and paced in his bedroom, put his ear up to the door, tried to figure out what was happening. His stomach did cartwheels. Then all of a sudden... nothing. Silence. He held his breath. Waited.

A knot developed in the pit of his stomach. He doubled over. Mother rushed in to tell him, but he already knew. His father had died. Mother said it was a heart attack.

It was his fault. Mother and his father fought over him. It broke his father's heart.

Noah woke up, gasped for air. Beads of perspiration dotted his forehead.

Kadee still lay asleep, scrunched up behind him. He kissed her hands, then moved them away from his face and down to his chest, right against his heart. Tears dripped down his cheeks.

Things with Kadee had moved along briskly. As it turned out, Kadee was easy to be with. Despite his best efforts to keep Kadee at a safe distance, Noah found himself spending a lot of time with her. Too much time, really. He remained embattled in an internal tug-of-war, trying his best to pull back whenever he felt himself developing deep emotions.

Meanwhile, he continued to see his relationship with Yvonne as just friends, which is what he had convinced himself was their current situation. They had kissed a few more times, passionate, loving exchanges, which gave him hope that Yvonne might be coming around. Finally, she would give him another chance. Noah spent the winter months balancing time with Yvonne with time with Kadee.

Did he feel confused?

Yeah, he did. If he was being honest with himself, he had a bad feeling about the whole thing right from the beginning. If Yvonne found out about Kadee, he would lose his chance to be with the only woman he ever really loved. But being with Kadee made him feel so incredibly masculine, so powerful. Like he was his own person, free of Mother. She was addictive.

Yvonne always made things difficult. Like she was some big award that had to be won only after years and years and *years* of hard work and, even with all his efforts, she still wasn't a sure thing.

Kadee made it easy. That both allured him and terrified him. The woman made it so easy, he couldn't be sure if he really meant something to her, or he was just some guy she'd have for the year. Would she dump his ass for the next guy who came along once she got bored of him? Women like Kadee do that. Women like Kadee ate men like him for breakfast. Besides, he never let her see inside him, how broken he was. He never told her about Mother. Once he did, if he did, she would probably run away from him as fast as she could.

Yvonne knew him. He trusted her with his life and his heart.

If only she wouldn't behave like she was an achievement award. Guilt: a wasted emotion. So on the occasion when it seeped into his consciousness, he would tell himself that this whole thing with Kadee, *whatever it was,* was Yvonne's fault.

If she didn't make it so difficult, this never would have happened.

Sometimes he wished he could shut off his desire to even be with a woman. He'd live his life alone, celibate, safe, a nice quiet life uncomplicated by the female gender.

No matter what, he would always have to deal with Mother, though. Unless he moved to another country, changed his name, his appearance, his whole identity, she would never let him be.

Mother would find him no matter where he went or what he did.

Noah fell back to sleep with Kadee wrapped around him. It was a light sleep, the kind where he felt half awake. He feared the memories: like an alligator hiding in a serene lake, those memories would creep out from under the surface and devour him whole if he let his mind ease with a false sense of security.

Mother called every weekend morning. The woman must have had "call Noah and be an impossible nuisance" in her calendar because she never missed a call. That call was the most reliable and predictable part of his day. Sometimes when he was in bed alone on a weekend morning, he would stare at the clock and fume, while he waited for the phone to ring. Mother could do that to a person: be so predictably annoying and overbearing that a person would come to depend on her.

Mother's call time was 9:30 a.m. Often Kadee and he would be in the middle of sex when Mother's calls came. He always answered her calls. The woman would have a conniption if he didn't. Mother's conniptions were not something that passed quickly. For days, she would go on a tirade about Noah's lack of appreciation, his disrespect of her, his impetuous disregard of her needs and feelings. Invariably she'd say something like: "Noah dear, you are an imprudent, ungrateful boy. Mother is the only person who really loves you. You must never take her for granted." It would roll off her tongue with the grace of a ballerina — or the hiss of a serpent.

"Yes, mother. I'm sorry." He would apologize, even though he wasn't sorry at all. Mother had to be appeased or she would never shut the fuck up.

Saturday morning. The sun glowed behind the monotonous, gray January sky, a tease of light through the heavy haze. Noah gazed out the window. He hated when the sun shined against an overcast sky creating a white, blinding glare while the ball of yellow remained hidden, a tantalizing possibility without promise. Maybe it would poke through; maybe it wouldn't. That type of sun was as capricious as a woman.

Kadee stirred under the comforter, noticed him by the window. "It's cold. Come lay with me."

Her dark hair sat on top of her head in a ponytail. When he looked at her, he saw innocence in her eyes, a vulnerability. He enjoyed when Kadee had that expression, but it never lasted. As soon as he embraced her, that flirtatious, confident way about her, would become prominent. And he would remember that she was unsafe — as fickle as the sun that January morning. She would tease him until he believed she would be his. He felt sure that once she knew she had him, she would swallow him whole, eat him up, then toss out all the broken, chewed-up pieces of his heart in one careless blink of an eye.

He returned to bed. Her body felt warm. Those rounded, *bunk-bunk* hips were bare under the comforter. He loved when Kadee lay naked next to him. Without her clothes on, she seemed more vulnerable. He felt more in control. In fact, a lot of the time he slept in boxers while she lay naked beside him. She seemed to enjoy being naked, which both aroused him and terrified him. A woman that comfortable in her nakedness was never to be trusted.

And Kadee was not shy when it came to her sexuality. Noah really enjoyed *that*. In fact, he would get her to dance naked for him. She would peal her clothing off slowly, as he asked, making sure to leave her panties for the end. He liked when she pulled them off gradually, exposing the triangle of her pubic hair last. After, when she stood naked, she would swirl around in a slow, tantalizing, erotic dance. Those *bunk-bunk* hips, her little waist, and that small triangle of pubic hair, belonged to him. In those moments, he felt the command of his virility. It was intoxicating.

Kadee was intoxicating.

When she was done, he would remember to lock the door to his heart, tight. There was a limit to what he would let himself feel for Kadee. As soon as he felt any sense of falling, that free exhilaration of giving his heart, that plummet into the abyss of love, he zipped his feelings back up as tight as he could, shutting down any possibility. Sometimes when he felt particularly at risk for feeling something for Kadee, he would imagine Yvonne's face, that pure admiration she had when she saw him. It always worked to seal whatever possible opening there was for Kadee. He couldn't let her in any of the cracks that remained opened.

But he enjoyed Kadee. Despite his best efforts, he practically couldn't resist her.

It was Kadee's fault that he struggled to fight off his infatuation. If she wasn't so sexual, so desirable, it never would have gotten this far.

He scooped his hands around her ass, and pulled her on top of him. He was already erect and slipped easily inside of her. He pulled the comforter off so he could watch her naked body go back and forth along him. He held her *bunk-bunk* hips tight, and watched her nipples harden. Her mouth hung open, her lower lip full and juicy, as she groaned. "Uh, uh, uh, keep going, that feels great baby."

He pushed harder, the sounds of her pleasure enveloping him. In that moment, there was nothing but Kadee and him and the movement of their bodies connected to each other.

Then...

Brrrring. Brrrriing. Brrrring. Mother. Right on time. He didn't even have to look at his phone. The ring felt violent and intrusive, exactly the way mother wanted it to feel.

"Your mother?" Kadee asked. She had become accustomed to his mother's weekend calls.

"Yep."

"Don't get it. Just this once, don't get it." She sat on him, naked, while he was inside of her. Her eyes pleaded.

He pulled her torso against his, and moved up and down in rhythm with her. "OK."

"I love you," she whispered in his ear.

"Love you, too." He responded without even thinking. In fact, in that fleeting, erotic-filled moment, he did love her. Man, did he love her. He pulled her closer.

An hour later, they lay half-asleep, bodies entwined. When...

Bang. Bang. Bang.

A series of fierce knocks sounded at Noah's front door, then the jingle of a key turning.

Noah jumped up, a bundle of nerves, and threw on pajama bottoms and a T-shirt. "It's Mother. Stay here." His body stiffened, his eyes hauntingly expressionless.

Noah got to the front door just as Mother slammed the door behind her. "Thank goodness you're alright. Mother called and called. When you didn't answer, I thought something terrible had happened."

"I'm fine, Mother."

She looked at him curiously. His T-shirt was wrinkled and his dark hair stood up all over. "What were you doing?"

"Sleeping."

"It's 10:30. It's unusual for you to sleep late." She moved toward the living room.

He stood in front of her, stopping her from moving further into his apartment.

"You have a woman here. Don't you."

"Y – Yes. Please go. I will call you in an hour. She's leaving."

Mother's eyes looked feral when she said, "Who is she? Not someone Mother introduced you to. A woman that I introduced you to wouldn't be over in the morning hours. After a sleepover, I'm assuming."

"Her name is Kadee. She's thirty-five, lives in the neighbor. She's a friend, Mother. It's nothing serious."

"You don't think sleeping over is serious. Mother really worries about you. And thirty-five is too old. She'll be fat and barren within a few years."

"Mother. Please. Lower your voice. Do not embarrass me. Please."

"You must listen to Mother. Mother loves you. Women can be manipulative and deceitful. You mustn't trust women.

The wrong woman could destroy your life. I am only looking out for you. You are my baby boy. I don't want to see a woman take advantage of you or hurt you. Mother will find you a nice woman."

"Yes. I understand."

"Make sure you get rid of that slut now. We're meeting for brunch at twelve-thirty. Remember?"

"Yes." He kissed her cheek, gently guided her toward the door. "See you then." He opened the door and put on a magnanimous smile.

He wanted to fling her into the hallway.

She lingered for a moment. Of course. God forbid she ever made anything easy. She pierced him with her eyes and in an overly graceful voice said, "She's leaving. Correct? Mother's worried."

"Yes. She's leaving."

"See you at twelve-thirty."

"See you then."

Her heels clacked her way down the hall.

Finally.

He ran his hand through his hair, pulling it back. As he watched her leave, he thought, *I hate you.*

He felt sure that he would one day explode into a violent outburst. Mother could do that to someone: push them right over the edge into fierce insanity.

His eyes still held a vacant look when he returned to the bedroom.

"What was that about?" Kadee's eyes looked troubled.

He could not deal with another woman's emotions right then. He felt sick looking at Kadee. He needed to be alone.

"Nothing, I don't want to talk about it." He said in a hollow voice. He wouldn't meet her eyes, but he sensed her neediness. She wanted to know what was wrong with him. Fuck her; it was none of her business. Besides, he felt that creepy-dirty feeling under his skin. Without another word, he left her alone in the bedroom and went into the shower. Steaming hot water cascaded over his body for over an hour.

"I have to go out," he said to Kadee when he got out of the shower. He stood with a towel around his waist, his hair wet. "I'll call you later." His manner was still flat.

"What's wrong. Tell me."

"Kadee. Stop. There's nothing to talk about it. Don't be needy. I'll call you later."

Stunned, Kadee snapped her head back. "Needy?!"

"I'm sorry." He looked her straight in the eyes. And he could see she was hurt. No doubt because he wasn't answering her question. A woman like Kadee didn't like not getting her way. He needed her to leave. Jumbled thoughts swarmed around his head, all tangled up and inarticulate. All he knew was he needed time alone. Kadee must leave, or he might blow a gasket. Bad enough he only had an hour before he had to share a meal with Mother.

In a steady and firm voice, trying his best to be considerate — not because he actually gave a shit about Kadee's needs in the moment, rather as an attempt to prevent her hurt feelings from escalating into elaborate hysteria — he said, "I'm meeting Mother for brunch. As you can see, she can be difficult. Please. I need some time to myself before I meet her."

"I gottcha. No problemo."

She seemed so casual. It irritated the shit out of him.

She cared, then just like that she didn't care. *I gottcha. No problemo.* What kind of careless, inconsiderate response was that? After he gave thought to his response to her, she gave none to him. Bitch.

"Love you." She kissed his cheek.

"Love you, too." He had to say it back or she would linger by the door waiting for him to say it. She probably only said it so he would say it back. Kadee probably didn't even mean it. He shot her a generous smile, even though underneath he was seething.

She left. Thank God for small things.

CHAPTER 8

Mid-March. The weather still had that gray, wintery feel, but the promise of spring hung in the air. The streets had patches of dirty snow so black it was hard to distinguish from tar. Noah walked through Central Park a few days a week, most times with Yvonne. In the park, the snow was still white. It hugged the bare trees and bordered the dirt trails. He enjoyed strolling through the park. A few times, Yvonne entwined her fingers in his and swung their hands as they walked along.

Noah feared he would run into Kadee. While holding Yvonne's hand, his eyes would dart around the park on vigilant guard. Yvonne must have sensed his angst because a few times she had asked if he was alright. She gave him a look, like she knew he wasn't alright, but would respect his privacy if he didn't want to share. Yvonne was great like that. She always read when he wasn't in the mood to talk. And she never pushed him.

Consequently, it was easy to respond with, "I'm fine." He'd get no histrionic song-and-dance from her. She'd just nod. He'd squeeze her hand. They would continue to walk.

Mother continued to harangue him about Kadee. Following her intrusion in January, he told Mother that he wasn't seeing Kadee anymore. But Mother knew he was lying. The woman knew everything. So he told her Kadee was a friend, an in-the-meantime woman, someone to spend time with until Mother found him a proper woman. He assured Mother that his relationship with Kadee wasn't sexual.

Why that was any of Mother's business was beyond Noah's comprehension. But when it came to Mother, it was futile to try to make sense of anything.

He would never date anyone Mother set him up with. But he would keep dishing out what she wanted to hear to keep her under control. Mother continued to berate him about Kadee, and he continued to say they were friends, nothing more.

She seemed to know he was being dishonest, but he told himself there was no way she could know the truth. Even Mother couldn't know what went on behind closed doors. If nowhere else, he had privacy in his bedroom.

Things with Kadee were… complicated. He knew he needed to break it off. Yet, every time he intended to have the "it was fun while it lasted conversation" the words would not come. He'd look into her eyes, a lump would develop in his throat, and he couldn't say it.

He didn't love her, really. He loved being with her. Passionate, intellectually challenging, even funny, Kadee was easy to be with. Plus, her sexual openness excited him.

Attracted him.

Angered him.

A few times when he sensed her wanting more from him, he felt like he hated Kadee. He hated her for making him want her so much. Fucking hated her. But then she'd act playful and easy-going, again, and his passion for her would erase any contempt — temporarily.

If he was really honest, Kadee made him feel nuts.

But he had *it* and *her* under control. Every time he felt reeled in, he pulled back, told himself: *You got this, Donovan.*

It was late March when his Kadee saga became more convoluted.

A Sunday morning. Sun streamed into Noah's apartment. A breeze blew through his opened windows, the curtains frolicking waves of cotton in the kitchen and living room. Noah ate his cereal and read the paper. Kadee sat beside him reading a book. A comfortable silence between them.

When he heard Kadee say, "Noah," with hesitancy in her voice, almost a tremble, he knew it was trouble. A woman saying a man's name with a cracking voice foreshadowed trouble. He looked up at her, half expecting tears to be gushing out of her eyes. She would employ the unscrupulous use of tears; try to get him to meet some superfluous need she had, no doubt.

But when he looked at those green eyes staring at him, they looked almost pained. He wondered if she knew about Yvonne. Not that there was anything to know, really. Sure, he kissed Yvonne a few times and they were getting closer. Noah believed consummation was soon approaching.

But nothing had happened yet. Besides, he never promised Kadee exclusivity.

"What is it, DeeDee?" He had taken to calling her, DeeDee, sometimes. His pet-name for her. She lit up whenever he said it. He thought it made her feel a special bond between them. Pet names often did that for women.

Then she said *it*.

Shit.

"I… well, I… find myself in unfamiliar territory. I find myself, um … wondering if we are in an exclusive relationship. We have never really talked about it."

Think, Donovan.

"No, we haven't had that conversation, have we? Well, what do *you* want, Kadee?" The full name was better for serious talks, such as a "where is this going" conversation.

Shit.

"I guess I assumed we were exclusive. I haven't been with anyone else, nor do I want to be. I'm hoping you feel the same."

Women. Never satisfied.

He took her hand, gave her his most endearing look, then shot her his magnanimous smile. "Of course, Kadee. I love you. I thought that was obvious. I'm sorry if it wasn't."

He embraced her tightly. *I do love you.* Caressed her neck with his lips. *Fucking bitch.*

He grabbed her face and planted a kiss on her lips, pushed his erection against her. He wanted her. He slowly removed her clothing, kissing her neck and shoulders as he undressed her, then he guided her into his bedroom.

After Kadee left that day, he swore to himself that he would create distance between them. He didn't want to end it, but he didn't want anything serious with Kadee, either. He would never be serious with Kadee. He wasn't even sure why anymore; he just knew she wasn't right, and she wasn't safe. Anything she did that made her seem vulnerable felt unscrupulous and manipulative. When she asked for anything, she felt demanding and needy. And the worst: When she seemed casual and easy-going, he started to become irritated, even angry, thinking that frivolous Kadee used him like some boy-toy and couldn't take *him* seriously.

Sometimes he really fucking hated her.

Chapter 9

Noah tried his best to keep his distance from Kadee, but it wasn't easy. As soon as she called, he would find himself calling back. If she stopped calling him so much, maybe he could stay away from her.

And what was his problem, anyway?

This should not be a problem for him. He controlled the intimacy, not her.

He could call the whole thing off whenever he wanted to. He just didn't want to... *yet*. With that, he decided rather impetuously to invite Kadee on a short trip to Fort Lauderdale. He had to go for a conference; he thought it would be fun to have her along. Besides, she kept giving him those pleading eyes, indicating that he wasn't providing whatever it was that she needed emotionally — he assumed. The trip would be something. A generous effort on his part.

The trip started out nice, too nice, actually. Kadee was inconveniently easy to be with. While he was busy at the conference, she did her own thing: studied, hung out on the beach, did yoga. She almost seemed not to care if he was there or not. Meanwhile, he found himself thinking about her alone on the beach, anticipating when he could leave the conference to be with her.

Thoughts about Kadee annoyed him, and he could not understand why the hell images of her intruded his mind. He wasn't in love with her; it was never going to be serious. He would never marry a woman like Kadee. Yet, he felt as pulled to her as a compass arrow to the North Pole.

He hated her for it. Her sexuality, her carelessness, her independence, her subversiveness. It was her fault.

Kadee was a seductress, and she had roped him in. He needed to regain control.

So, on the third night he insisted they go to a strip club. She seemed reticent at first. He remained gently persistent. He could see the waver in her eyes. If he pushed just a little more, she would give in.

And she did.

Good thing. He wanted her to see what real whores looked like. If she wanted to act like a whore, using her sexuality to exploit and control men — him — then she should see how it was done correctly.

She was an amateur.

The women in the strip club loved him. He held the money up, and they flocked over, putty in his hands. He taunted them with fives, tens and twenties. Got them to spread their legs, bend over, all those vulnerable female positions that let him see who they really were. He sat fully clothed and watched them show him their everything.

The money controlled those women. The more he dished out, the more they exposed. He always reveled in his relationships with whores, April in particular. It was the most genuine relationship a man could have with a woman. Since the sex was a given, there were no games, no manipulations, no problems.

Besides, when it came to the whores, he always controlled them with his money. Money did that to people. His mother always used his father's money to control Noah. He learned the value of financial power and superiority from the best: Mother.

Kadee tugged on him a few times, seeming uncomfortable. She asked to leave. That irritated him. He was on a high, couldn't she see that. "Just a little while longer." He smiled wide, kissed her cheek. He wondered how anyone as sexually adventurous and open as Kadee could be such a prude when it came to strippers.

"Alright." She took a heavy breath, crossed her arms around her chest, sunk back into her chair.

He ordered her another vodka cranberry. "Here. After this drink."

She took it. Her lips bunched up in one corner, clearly perturbed.

Less than ten minutes later, she said, "Listen. I'm going. If you want to stay, fine. I'll take a taxi."

Noah felt heat course through his body. She was acting independent as a way to manipulate him. She was using the threat of leaving on her own to get him to leave. It infuriated him. He looked at her through cold eyes, slammed his drink on the bar, and in a raised voice said, "Fine."

There was no conversation between them the entire car ride back to the hotel, only the heavy silence of unspoken words.

Noah had never raised his voice to Kadee like that before. The woman was really starting to get to him. She brought out a side of him that he didn't like.

When they got back to the hotel room, he cracked a bottle of tequila, poured two shots. He tried to gauge her emotional state. She took the drink, searched his face.

"I'm sorry." He apologized and kissed her cheek.

She nodded and gave him a pursed-lipped smile. The heavy look in her eyes lightened. She started to change into her nightgown.

"Dance for me." He plopped on the bed, rested his head back on the headboard.

She looked surprised.

"Come on, DeeDee, you know those women mean nothing to me. You're the only one I want to see dance."

Puckered lips, one eye squinted, she implored him with a "you must be kidding me" face. Kadee always indulged him sexually, but this look of defiance beseeched him to stop asking. He worried if he had crossed a line with her, one that could not be uncrossed. He did not want to lose Kadee... *yet.*

Part of him could not stand her for it.

He hated her for making him want her.

"Com'ere. I'm sorry." He pulled her down next to him on the bed. Stiff and tense, she laid next to him. He stroked her hair, gently kissed her neck, whispered, "I'm sorry. I love you." Finally, she relaxed against him, and he knew through her body language that she forgave him.

An hour later, Kadee slept soundly. Noah envied her ability to plop into a deep sleep. Sleeping never came easily for him. Half the time he wondered if he would ever have a full night sleep.

On the precipice of sleeping and wakefulness, his arms around Kadee, those hollow children's voices started singing: *Noah and Belle sitting in a tree K-I-S-S-I-N-G. First comes love, then comes the berry, then comes daddy in the cemetery.*

He rustled on the bed, placed his hand across his brow, squeezing, hoping the images of his father dead on the kitchen floor wouldn't come. That was the worst day of his life: The day his father died. He blamed himself. Mother had been crawling into bed with him, pushing her naked body against his for four years. This time his father saw. Now, he would leave mother and take Noah with him. It was Noah's fault. Mother always said, "Thank goodness Mother has you. You are the love of Mother's life."

It felt weird when Mother said it while she lay pressed against him in his bed. Part of him sensed it was wrong for some reason. Now as a man he understood what Mother did, laying with him like that, pushing her naked body against him, he knew it wasn't something a Mother did with her son. However, at the time, all he felt was confused, excited, sick. Guilty.

Guilty for causing problems between Mother and his father; if his father left, it would be because of Noah.

Guilty, because he had let Mother curl up with him; he should have stopped it.

Guilty, because a part of him felt aroused by it, her attention made him feel special, loved. A few times he remembered waiting with eagerness for her to come into his bed. At the same time as he anticipated her arrival with a quiet zeal, he despised her presence. And he despised himself even more for being aroused by her — his own mother. If his father left, it would be because he knew a part of Noah enjoyed feeling Mother's nakedness beside him, the purr of her breath blowing softly into his ear, their special bond. A number of times he threw up from thinking about the moments of closeness they shared and the way his penis expanded while she lay next to him.

When Mother came into his room that day his father had a heart attack, she had said, "He never should have threatened to leave and take you, my baby boy, with him."

Tears had gushed down Noah's cheeks. *It's my fault.* At first, he thought his relationship with mother killed his father.

But then his friend Max found those berries, and everything got worse.

Worried that it was one of those awful nights when his mind would remain preoccupied with those dark memories, those memories he tried to block out, but couldn't, he kissed Kadee's cheek and slipped out of bed.

He went down to the hotel pool to swim — to submerge his body in water.

Chapter 10

Back in New York after the Fort Lauderdale trip, Noah's life took a sharp turn down an unexpected path. Yvonne's thirty-ninth birthday. Noah took her out. *No big deal*, he thought as he ambled over to her office to pick her up.

When she walked out, he knew he was in trouble. Her dark hair hugged her shoulders and cascaded in tendrils down her back over her sleek, black dress. Red lipstick highlighted her pouty lips. Yvonne always wore tailored clothes. Always in good taste. She never dressed sexy. Just collared shirts, pressed slacks or a straight knee-length skirt, *maybe* a fitted sweater or cotton shirt. Often, a pony tail innocently frolicked back and forth as she walked. That was Yvonne's usual for as long as he had known her.

Tonight, she looked different, striking, even sensual.

Problem was, Noah knew as soon as he laid eyes on her that she wanted to look good *for him*. This wasn't a friend taking another friend out for a birthday celebration. This was a date. A date Noah had waited for. His neck perspired under his shirt.

He tugged at his collar, opened a second button. The air suddenly felt thick with the heat of sex.

"Hi handsome." She placed her hand delicately in his.

He squeezed her hand, kissed her cheek. "Beautiful birthday girl." A sweet smell filled his nose. Yvonne was wearing a new perfume. This was definitely a date.

She blushed, gave a coquettish smile.

"So where are you taking me?"

"Downtown."

They walked to the corner. Noah's arm waved wildly as he tried to hail a cab.

"You OK? You seem… tense or rushed. Are we late for a reservation?"

"No. Sorry. I'm just excited to get there."

She cocked her head, an eyebrow raised, like she didn't believe him. But she let it go.

Standing on her corner made him tense. If Kadee happened to stroll by, he was totally screwed. They had only arrived back from Florida the day before. She had called him, too; he still hadn't returned her calls. He knew not returning a woman's call was never a wise choice. The absence of explanations from departures of the regular relationship rhythm could turn an otherwise steady woman into a psycho.

He would call her tomorrow.

Finally, a taxi came. The duo slid in. Noah relaxed back into the seat.

Being with Yvonne was always so uncomplicated. She understood him, especially his need for space, and he could confide in her. He could always tell her the truth about himself. But now he had a secret. A big fat secret, one that he had been able to rationalize until that night at dinner. But now, that big, fat secret was a big, fat problem.

However, if he didn't consummate his relationship with Yvonne, take it to the next level, he believed wholeheartedly he would have done nothing wrong. He would break it off with Kadee, then start it up with Yvonne.

But as the evening continued, he knew she was waiting for him to make the first move. That purposeful demure look in her blue eyes, the way her hand stayed on his arm while she looked at him, then looked away, then looked back, he would have to be totally obtuse not to see what she wanted.

If he didn't do it tonight, he might lose his chance. Yvonne was a no-nonsense sort of gal. If he blew it with her, another chance might never come.

Later, they got out of the taxi around the corner from Yvonne's. Noah felt tense. The Upper Eastside always seemed big, but it was small. For an urban atmosphere, it was amazing how easily gossip traveled around the neighborhood. Not so smart to take it up with two women who lived within a half mile of each other. And of course, there was Mother living nearby too, up his ass and as relentless as a starving cat first thing in the morning.

In front of Yvonne's apartment, the crossroad lay before him. He knew his decision. He wanted to be with her. In that moment, he felt swept away by the vulnerability he saw in her eyes. Two huge pools of blue begged him to say yes when she asked, "You want to come in for a bit?"

Their eyes locked. He nodded.

With his arm wrapped around her petite frame, they walked into her building, went up in the elevator through the hallway into her apartment.

Noah stayed over Yvonne's that night. Naked bodies woven comfortably together, it felt so good to finally have her next to him.

Finally, he had made love with Yvonne.

Then…

Vvvvvt. Vvvvvt. Vvvvvt.

His phone vibrated.

"Who is that, handsome? Please tell me your mother isn't calling after midnight."

Vvvvvt.

He looked at the screen: Kadee.

Ding.

A voicemail. Her second one.

He'd listen to her messages in the morning.

He'd end it with Kadee in the morning.

He shut his phone off, whispered, "Yeah. It's mother. I shut it off so we could be alone."

"Good." She squeezed him.

Chapter 11

Women are fickle.
The morning after, 9:12 a.m., and he had just gotten home from Yvonne's.

Before he left, Yvonne had explained that they had to take things *sloooow*. She still wasn't sure if she could trust him with her heart.

What the fuck?

It had been thirteen years

Thirteen years of trying to make up for an error of youth and immaturity.

He had been waiting and waiting, hanging around like some pathetic stray cat hoping the butcher would toss out some scraps. He would take whatever he could from Yvonne, even if it was less than what he wanted just to have a tiny piece of her. An itsy-bitsy piece as she would say. When Yvonne used itsy-bitsy, he knew she was ticked off. That was her angry phrase.

Yvonne was weird.

So, Yvonne, maybe I'm just an itsy-bitsy bit angry at your capricious nature.

Meanwhile, Kadee's messages sounded panicked *and* intrusive. Exactly like Mother's messages always did, when — God forbid — he didn't answer her calls fast enough. Kadee acted concerned with the *"Where are you? It's not like you not to call. I hope everything's OK. "*

Meanwhile, he felt confident that Kadee actually didn't give a shit where he was. She wasn't worried if he was OK. Kadee simply wanted to intrude upon his privacy, know where he was and what he'd been up to.

The only thing that could ever really make a man *not* OK was a woman.

He learned exactly what women were capable of from Mother. A sad truth. One he tried his best to block out. His education in the violent proclivities of a scorned female came when Max found the berries.

Women 101:

Max found berries, plump violet berries, loads of them, in a Mason jar in the pantry.

The day after his father's funeral, while Mother was at the doctor, his mother's friend Sundae came over with her son, Max, to watch Noah. Max was one grade ahead of Noah. Tall, with a tuft of orange hair, and a face splattered with freckles, Max was always getting into trouble. Not a terrible kid, just a little bit of a rebel.

Noah liked him.

Max took the jar of berries off the shelf, unscrewed the lid. Noah and he were about to dive in when Sundae walked in the room. She casually glanced at them, then stopped in her tracks as a look of horror spread across her face. She yelled, "Nooooo!" then lunged for the jar and snatched it from Max's hands.

"What?" Max looked bewildered. "They're fruit, mom."

"They are rotten fruit." She placed the jar on the counter and pulled back her long hair —the same orange hair as Max, thick and pin-straight — into a tight ponytail. Her big blue eyes looked frantic as she got to work emptying the jar into the sink.

Max gave her a confused smirk. "They don't look rotten to me."

"Take my word for it. They're no good." She glanced over at Noah, then averted her gaze as she wondered if he knew the truth behind the berries. Her hands shook as she diligently made sure that every single berry was ground up in the garbage disposal in the kitchen sink.

Max must have told some of the other boys at school because people started to talk about these poisonous berries. The stir of gossip among neighbors traveled quickly. Whispering voices, severe gazes, and synthetic smiles, appeared everywhere Noah went.

He started to hear the buzz of whispers in his sleep. No one would tell him the truth. Mother's adult friends told him that they were only rumors. "Children will be children.

They're just being mean." Sundae had said one day. Noah had stayed with her and Max while Mother was in the hospital with her "illness."

Mother had had a breakdown. She tried to hang herself and went into the loony bin, he later found out.

But the kids at school teased him something awful. They sang about the berries. The hum of vicious voices echoed every time he had to go through the hallway.

"*Your mama killed your papa. Nah, nah, nah. I heard it's because your mama loved you instead of your papa. Nah, nah, nah.*"

One burly seventh-grade boy called Trucker taunted him relentlessly. He would follow Noah through the halls, into the bathroom, around the neighborhood and sing in a high-pitched, mocking tone: "Yo, Donovan, I heard you tongue-kissed your mother. Is it true, Noah dear? Did you kiss yo mama? Yo mama must not have liked your kisses, 'cause she tried to kill herself. Dangling Donovan. Ahahaha." He released a long and scathing laugh, whenever he called Noah's mother, Dangling Donovan. It made Noah's hair stand on end.

That same burly kid made up that dreadful song that he could never quite erase from his mind: "Noah and Belle sitting in a tree K-I-S-S-I-N-G" wouldn't stop playing in his head.

It felt like the song was blasting from loudspeakers everywhere.

Synchronized voices, fierce faces, and violent laughter menaced him. Even when he wasn't at school, he saw those kids singing at him. Taunting him in his thoughts. He cried himself to sleep every night. A couple times he thought of drinking something under Sundae's sink that had a warning about being poisonous if ingested.

As soon as Mother got out of the hospital, they left Boston and moved to New York City to start over.

The idea that his mother killed his father was too much to bear, so he told himself it was an impossible truth. And he all but buried it. Until one day Mother told him a new version of the story.

Chapter 12

He waited two more days to return Kadee's phone calls. Heaven forbid a man should want a little space. The woman kept calling and texting, an endless recital of faux concern. *"I'm really worried."* One text had said.

Mother used those exact words when he tried to take some time for himself.

Part of him enjoyed knowing Kadee needed him, part of him felt strangled by it.

Finally, he sent a text: *Sorry, DeeDee. Been crazy at work. Exhausted. Dinner tomorrow night?*

A half hour later she responded: *Yes. Sounds good.*

Of course, nothing was that simple.

The next day, Yvonne called in the afternoon, asking to see him. *Fickle,* he thought, irritated as he listened to her willowy voice say, "I'm sorry if I'm being difficult. I do miss you, though. Come for lunch?"

"I can't today. I'm busy with patients. No time for lunch."

A pause. Then... "Come over tonight? I mean, if you want. Sorry it's so last minute."

The questioned dangled in the air. He could envision those big baby blues wide and exposed as she waited on the line hoping — praying — he'd say yes.

"I have dinner plans with a colleague. After that?"

"OK. Sounds good, handsome. Just text when you're on your way. Tootles."

"Alright. See you."

He compiled a text to Kadee: *Hi DeeDee. Sorry, something came up. Dinner tomorrow, instead?*

After contemplating for a minute, he deleted the message. No reason he couldn't end the dinner early with Kadee, then go to Yvonne's. After Kadee's string of calls and texts, he thought she might flip out if he cancelled. Why he cared was beyond his comprehension. He planned to end it, anyway. But, for whatever obscure reason, he couldn't end it. Not yet.

Whenever he thought *I will end it today,* he found himself calling her, even making plans with her. Whatever it was about Kadee, his desire to have her overpowered his conscious thoughts, even his intentions. The more he tried not to think about her, the more he did.

And he hated her for it.

Dinner with Kadee was pleasant, too pleasant, really. He found his hand resting on top of hers as she spoke about her week. He hoped she would pressure him, ask him where he had been, why he hadn't called. This way he could be furious at her for pushing him, suffocating him, being the demanding, whining, nagging woman he knew she was under that coat of armor she wore. Nothing.

In fact, she seemed relaxed, calm, cool, even happy. It started to fucking annoy him halfway through dinner. Like mother, she truly didn't care where he had been or if he *was doing* OK. The quiver in her voice on the phone, that concerning tone she affected when she had said *"I hope you're OK,"* was just a way to control him.

Underneath his generous smile and warm eyes… he stewed.

She swirled the wine in her glass, said, "So, I'm reading *Crime and Punishment.* Have you read it?" Her green eyes held a curious look. Kadee sometimes enjoyed these heady, intellectual conversations. An attractive little trait of hers, and he enjoyed hearing her talk about her interests in psychology and literature. He had spent his career surrounded by science-minded folks, which was his forte. Kadee held a breadth of knowledge that he had never been exposed to in another person. And the way she dissected things was remarkably astute. Undeniably sexy, the flow of expansive knowledge flew off her tongue, confidently, and she looked pensive, even emotive. As he watched her lips, he kept thinking of holding those *bunk-bunk* hips. How could a women as sexy and sexually expressive as her, someone as knowledgeable and sharp-as-a-whip ever love him?

She didn't.

"No. I haven't. Studying medicine didn't leave a lot of time for deep reading of other disciplines. And now when I read, I'm either reading to keep up in my field or something light and easy."

"Yeah. I had a good friend in college who was premed. She never went out. Those lab reports alone were like a nightmare. As I've always told you, I give you a lot of credit. Medicine is not easy. Actually, a few of my friends dropped out after the first semester of organic chemistry."

"It was hard. But when you love something, it's not work, right." He smiled, and this time it felt genuine.

"I'll drink to that." She raised her glass and he raised his. *Click*.

"In *Crime and Punishment*, the protagonist kills two people. A few of my friends read it and recommended it. It's interesting to read a fictional perspective. I mean, I have interviewed murderers before, but it's always difficult to know if they are telling the truth about their remorse."

"Fiction isn't the truth. Isn't that the essence of fiction? It's made up." He chuckled.

"Yes and no. I think fiction tells the truth by not having to tell the truth." Noah gave her a skeptical look. She continued, "Authors tap into their unconscious, and the narrative spills out from the deepest recesses of their minds, tapping into motives, thoughts, feelings. All emblematic of something within the human condition. That's why good fiction resonates."

"Like the collective unconscious?" He smirked to himself, feeling clever. *I can be cerebral, too, Ka**dee**.*

"Yes. I forgot you had said you read some Jung."

"I'm full of surprises." He felt his eyes smile. He enjoyed Kadee.

Bitch.

After dinner he walked with her toward her apartment. He would leave her at her door, scoot over to Yvonne's. It was near 11:00 p.m. already. The dinner went longer than he had anticipated. Right before they left the restaurant, he had inconspicuously texted Yvonne that he would be there shortly.

She had responded: *See you soon J*

As they got closer to her apartment, Kadee picked a fight. Of course.

He should have known it was coming. God forbid she could let them have a nice evening without causing drama and conflict — her typical histrionics.

"Aren't we going back to your place?"

"Not tonight, babe. I have an early morning meeting. You know I'm a horrible sleeper. I want to at least try to get a good night sleep."

"That never bothered you before." Her voice had an uncharacteristic screech. It made his hair stand on ends.

"DeeDee, this is a really early morning meeting with the research team. I need to be fresh and rested to present my proposal." He had fabricated a research proposal earlier in the evening in case he needed to use it as an excuse. He'd tell Yvonne about the fictional research proposal, too.

"Noah. I know something is wrong. You're acting distant. Talk to me."

His chest tightened. "I don't need this, Kadee. What's gotten into you? This isn't like you. You're acting really needy. You know I don't like that."

"You're blaming this on me. You're the one who's been acting different."

"I've just been busy." There's the nagging wench. He knew she was under there.

"You've been distant. It's more than busy, isn't it?"

"Nope. Just busy. Really." *Don't roll your eyes, Donovan. She'll go nuts.*

Then with these sad puppy dog eyes and a long face she said, "OK. But if there is something, if something has changed for you, I want you to tell me. You would right?"

He barely looked at her. "Absolutely. Nothing has changed."

That really was the truth. Everything was the same as it had been from the beginning — for him, anyway. Kadee wanted more. She now wanted things he would not give her.

That's what changed.

She changed.

What *she* wanted changed. Not him. He was the same as he always had been. Why the fuck was she putting this on him?

Suffocation was an understatement. But to be respectful, which he always tried to be, he walked her home. He could feel her wanting to talk more about this fantasy that something was wrong with him, this fiction she created that he held back some coveted information. The air had a heavy feeling.

Finally, they arrived at her apartment. He kissed her, said, "I'll call you tomorrow."

She searched his face. He worried that she might slap him. Instead, she said, "OK," turned and walked up the stairs to her building.

OK. As if she weren't upset he was not coming up.

OK. As if she had not just made a big stink about him pulling back from her.

OK as if that fucking bitch was not playing games with him.

Well… fuck her. Noah had a booty call waiting for him. Noah did not require or welcome Kadee's mind games. She was toxic.

Noah loosened his collar, headed over to Yvonne's. Three avenues and four blocks from Kadee – NOT far enough.

Less than an hour later, he lay curled up in Yvonne's bed with her. He twirled her hair through his fingers.

She looked up at him batting her eyelashes. She whispered, "Do you love me?"

"You know I do."

"I like it when you *say* it."

"I love you, Yvonne."

She squeezed him.

"I want to marry you."

It just fell off his lips. It was the truth, though.

She kissed his lips. Then, staring into his eyes, she gave him that warm smile he loved.

He knew she would say yes, eventually; those sparkling baby blues told him so.

That night, Noah slept soundly, not waking up once.

In the morning, Yvonne shooed him out with, "I've got an early patient this morning. Sorry to have to rush you out."

He didn't want to leave her. He kept pulling her back for one more kiss. "Let's have dinner tonight."

"Oh, handsome, not tonight. OK? I am so enjoying our time. I really am. But I need to take things slow. I hope you understand."

Slow. It's been thirteen years.

"I do." He held both of her hands in his, looked at her face.

"I'll call you later, or call me. We'll figure out a time for dinner."

"Alright."

"Toodles."

As he strolled home in a reverie about the evening with Yvonne and how peaceful he felt sleeping next to her, he made the resolute decision to end it with Kadee. She was hot, but he did not need her mind games. Sure, Yvonne wanting to take things slow annoyed him, but in a way it was a good thing. It gave him time to break it off with Kadee before Yvonne and he took it to the next level of commitment:

engagement. He wanted Yvonne to be his fiancée. He would call Kadee later, ask her to dinner, break it off.

Their relationship — if you could even call fucking around without any emotional ties a "relationship" — had always had an expiration date, and that date had come. It was time. *No problem,* he thought, as he went into his apartment.

Chapter 13

Later that evening when he took Kadee for the breakup dinner, he ran into a snag. His words were stubborn and would not form on his tongue. They hung there all night as a possibility, but as he sat with her, talked, even laughed, the words escaped him. Then, like her little puppet, he found himself sleeping over her apartment.

The ceiling had a long crack in it right over her bed. He spent most of the night staring at it wondering what he was doing. He wanted to slip through that crack in the ceiling. Hide himself away. Disappear from Kadee's life, or make Kadee disappear from his. She was the root of all his troubles. If he wanted to be with Yvonne, he needed to end things with Kadee. How long could he pull this off? And how would it end? Yvonne already had difficulty trusting him. If she had even a miniscule suspicion of what he was up to, it was over.

He would make sure she never found out. And he would break it off with Kadee. Soon. Very soon.

Or as soon as Yvonne agreed to marry him or at least be in a committed relationship with him. When Yvonne stopped keeping him at arm's length, stopped trying to control his life with her wounded animal nonsense, then, he would end it with Kadee.

Easy. No problem. *You got this, Donovan.*

Noah rode that emotional roller coaster through the spring. He bounced back and forth between hanging out with Yvonne, mostly lunches in her therapy office, and time with Kadee. Meanwhile, the sex with Kadee was better than ever. It actually got better with time, which was not a good thing given the circumstances. But man, she was hot. Sexually vibrant and open. They had had a threesome with her neighbor one Saturday. It lasted all night. The other woman was also sexy and open. Another one of those women who strutted around with her bush hanging out like she hadn't an ounce of shame, the neighbor aroused him, too. He was forty years old and he had only just experienced the hottest sex of his life. It made him feel even more emotionally attached to Kadee, which was not good. He didn't have these kinds of feelings for Yvonne, and they were practically ready to marry. He loved Yvonne. Cared about her. But shouldn't he have passion for her? Was he making a mistake?

He felt tangled up, confused. So couldn't let Kadee go even if he wa made him hate her. In fact, the more he hated her.

Fucking hated her.

Then… like a train wreck, before he could slam on the brakes, one crash would lead to another. And another. A cascade of troubles, one crashing into the next.

The finale would not be good. He knew it even as he felt the train careening down the tracks. Yet, he felt helpless to stop it.

And he really had tried, hadn't he.

Kadee started the ball rolling with another impossible demand: She wanted him to meet her best friend, Vanessa. *Blah, blah, blah* was what he heard spewing from her mouth.

He ate his cereal, tried not to react to her.

"Are you listening to me? This is important." She placed her hands on those *bunk-bunk* hips and tilted her head, perturbed.

With a cold glare, he responded, "It's too soon."

Kadee looked exasperated. "Too soon? Eight months? Don't you think it's odd that we spend all of our time alone? I haven't met any of your friends, or you mine! Are you ashamed of me?"

"Stop pushing me, Kadee." He pulled the neck of his T-shirt down, rolled his neck.

pushing you? I never ask for anything." Kadee's voice pierced his ears.

"You're being needy, Kadee. I hate when you're needy. You know I hate that."

First her eyes watered, then tears gushed out. A melodramatic display used as an attempt to get what she wanted. Mother did that crap all the time — *all the time* — when he was a boy. And Mother's heart was as cold and bloodless as a stone. .

What was Kadee's problem anyway? Things were fine the way they were. Like meeting Vanessa was formal evidence of a more serious relationship? Women always pulled this kind of shit, which is why he never got too involved with any of them; except Yvonne, she never asked for anything.

I've got to break it off with Kadee. This is out of hand.

"I like things the way they are right now. Can't we just take it slow?"

Kadee cried into a napkin. Her head bowed, shoulders shaking. Her sobs filled the apartment.

She seemed upset. She did. Genuinely upset, but he just couldn't trust it. Trust her.

With a steady voice he said, "You're a mess, Kadee. Pull yourself together. Why are you crying? You're making things worse crying like a spoiled brat who's not getting her way. You're boxing me in." He pulled the neck of his T-shirt down so low, he nearly ripped it. He needed her to leave, but she didn't budge.

He went into his bedroom and slammed the door, leaving her and her ridiculous outburst in the kitchen. What on earth had her *this* upset? So, he didn't want to meet her friend Vanessa. Big deal.

Needy. So. Fucking. Needy.

He called his buddy Theo, made a plan to hang out. He needed an afternoon away from women, no Kadee, no Yvonne and NO Mother.

He went back into the kitchen. The tears had stopped, but Kadee's face looked long. Her eyes were red and puffy.

He took a heavy breath, not in the mood for more hysterics, he tried to be gentle. "I'm going out. I think we need a break today."

"What? Where are you going?" Her eyes held a desperate look, a soul-sucking "I need you in order to survive" look.

It made his hair stand on ends.

"Out with Theo."

She sniffled, trying to get him to dissect the disagreement they had. *Analyze our feelings? Is she insane?* He inched toward the door, showing her with his body language that he wanted her to leave. Hopefully, he wouldn't have to throw her out. That would be really ugly.

Kadee got up, slowly got her stuff together. He could tell she was taking her time, hoping he would say something, but he just watched her. He had nothing to say.

At the door, he kissed her, said, "I'll call you later. OK?"

"Sure."

Suddenly, she seemed all put together, like those tears were purposefully engineered — as he had suspected. Always suspected. Another manipulative lie. When the waterworks didn't get her what she wanted, she shut them off. No big deal for Kadee.

The door closed behind her. He waited for the squeak of her sneakers to fall away.

Not even a full minute later came the intrusive blare of Mother.

Brrrring Brrrring Brrrring

He knew it was her without even looking at the phone. Despite the fact that he used the same ringtone for all of his incoming calls, he could tell when it was Mother. As though she possessed some psychic power that could make her calls sound different only to him. The ringing pierced his ears like nails on a chalkboard.

He did not want to deal with her.

A heavy, sighing breath, then, "Yes, Mother."

"Hello, dear. Don't bring Yvonne to dinner tonight. Mother wants some time alone with you."

"But I've already confirmed our plans with her. What's the big deal?"

"It's just that Yvonne talks too much. It's impossible for us to really catch up when she's there. She drones on and on and– "

"Fine. Fine," he said in a defeated voice. He did not have the wherewithal to argue with mother today. "I'll come alone."

"Thank you, dear. Mother loves you. See you at *our* restaurant at 7:30."

"Alright. Bye, Mother."

He needed a few minutes to compose himself before calling Yvonne. He needed to figure out his deception should she put up a fight. Telling her that Mother was the reason could not happen. Women, he found, were exhausting.

He got on the phone with Yvonne. "Can we reschedule dinner tonight? I'm sorry."

"Your mother?"

"Um..." *How did she know? Perhaps Mother was not so subtle.*

"Of course. I understand. I really do... Are you OK? You sound exhausted."

Well, that was easy. Kadee should be this easy to manage. "I'm fine. Just the usual crap with her. She's exhausting."

"Oh, I know she is, handsome. You're such a good son. You really are. Just remember that."

"Dinner later in the week? Just me and you. I'll leave Mother at home."

"Yes. Give me a call or text, and we'll work it out."

"Great." His shoulders relaxed.

"And handsome... don't let her get to you. You know she can be merciless when she wants her way, but she does love you." *Yvonne really does know Mother. Who knew?*

"You're a gem. Love you."

"Thank you. Ta ta."

Still, Yvonne wouldn't say it back. Yvonne was not going to release the "I love you, too" easily. Would she ever?

Chapter 14

Dinner with Mother. They sat outside. Mother talked. He listened with one ear, let his second margarita drown out the irritation he felt. Homely Lillian Seasons was available, again. Hip hip hooray.

"Mother, I'm not interested."

"Please tell me it's not about that Kadee woman you were seeing. The one whose parents are teachers. I know she's slept over a bunch of times. Slut."

"Mother. She hasn't slept over in months. And no, it's not because of her. I'm forty years old. I'm not your little boy anymore. And I don't like Lillian."

"Noah, dear. You really worry mother. Lillian is a nice woman. And I know you're not being honest about Kadee. A mother knows these things." She raised one eyebrow.

She couldn't possibly know about Kadee.

But Mother held superior talent for making a person question their own reality. Nearly telepathic in her ability to know things impossible for her to know, mother was akin to an omniscient deity.

And as if she called Kadee through some bizarre psychic connection — if anyone held that talent, it would be Mother — Kadee suddenly appeared at their table.

Kadee stood right over him, a foreboding presence. He jumped in his seat

At first, he didn't trust his own eyes. Was that her standing beside him, crazed eyes, wild hair, tight lips? But as he glanced down and saw her hands placed threateningly on those *bunk-bunk* hips, he knew his eyes weren't deceiving him.

He stood up, fumbled on his words. "Um... Kadee... um... what are you doing here?" He looked at his ageless mother, who had a satisfied smirk on her painted red lips.

"I live here. What are you doing here?" Kadee looked at Mother, smiled, then looked back at him, her eyes furious.

His hand gently on her back, he attempted to guide her away from the table before she made a scene. He could see she was teetering on the brink of a freak-out. He felt it. "C'mon, DeeDee. Let's go over here to talk about it."

Kadee stood, determined in her spot beside the table. Noah tried to cajole her away. Kadee would not move.

Instead, she introduced herself to Mother.

Damn it, Kadee.

Mother pursued her crimson lips into a polite smile. The gleam of triumph exuded from her eyes. Her countenance screamed: *See Noah, dear, you can't hide anything from Mother. I knew about Kadee. Ha-ha-ha.*

His heart raced as he tried again to move Kadee away. The woman stood her ground, stubborn, arms folded across her chest in what appeared to be a standoff with his mother.

Kadee blurted, "Did you know that he is my boyfriend? Did you know that?"

No. No. Oh fuck!

"Friend," he exclaimed without thinking. He rested a hand on Mother's shoulder, hoping she wouldn't say something unabashed back to Kadee, humiliating him. Mother was capable of anything.

"Friend? Friend?" Kadee grew increasingly exacerbated. Those crazed eyes turned venomous. A slap threatened.

His mother looked entertained.

"Friend? You're freaking kidding me."

In one last fruitless attempt, he placed his hand on Kadee's back, nearly shoved her away from Mother and their table. Occupants of neighboring tables now turned their heads to watch the show.

Kadee took his drink off the table, her eyes frantic and feral. Her hand shook as she gripped that drink, contents spilling over the rim. She gave him one last harrowing glare, threw the drink in his face, slammed the glass on the table, then ran away from them.

Margarita dripped down his face. Dropped jaws and wide eyes stared from the adjacent tables.

Humiliated, furious, he went to go after her.

His mother pulled his shirt. "Let her go, dear." Those ruby lips puckered victoriously. "Let her go. You can call her tomorrow."

He stewed, but Mother pulled his arm and motioned him to sit. Kadee's display of hysterics was bad enough, he didn't want to have to manage backlash from Mother if he didn't follow her firm request. "OK, Mother." He felt like a loser; his mother's little pussy subordinate who would do whatever she wanted just to shut her the fuck up.

"I told you, dear. You need to break it off with her. And how did she not know who I was? She's at your apartment all the time. Mother's pictures are there. Does she go into the bedroom for sex and not observe any of her surroundings."

"Mother. Please. I do not want to talk about it. Kadee is oblivious. OK? And… I will end it. You're right. OK? Can we not talk about her?"

"Fine, dear. Here, let Mother clean your face." She licked her napkin, brought it to his face.

His cheeks burned from embarrassment. He looked out of his periphery to see if anyone was watching them.

A bald-headed guy with big blue eyes stared right at them.

"Mother. Please." He whispered, grabbing the napkin from her hand to wipe his own face.

She retracted her hand.

Thank God for small things. Although Mother rescinding wasn't really a small thing. The woman made a bull look as timid as a bunny.

He did have Mother to thank for one thing: Yvonne was not there. If it weren't for Mother, Yvonne would have been privy to the evening's exhibition, which included Kadee's disclosure that he was her boyfriend. It would have been difficult, if not impossible, to weasel his way out of that one.

Things were messy. The proximity between them all was way too small. A few blocks, a few avenues. It was only a matter of time before Yvonne found out. Things were too close for comfort. Maybe this was a sign that it was time to end it with Kadee.

He would call Kadee, explain the woman he was with was Mother, then break it off.

CHAPTER 15

Not tonight. Not yet. Not right after what happened.

He would wait until this incident blew over before he broke it off with Kadee. He made that decision by the time he had arrived home from dinner with his mother. Although he was pissed at Kadee, he could understand why she was upset. He owed it to her to explain that the woman was his mother.

Besides, he knew he frustrated Kadee. Theo had even said it that afternoon. "She's acting nuts because she wants more, and you're not giving it to her. Dude. You're staying with a woman who is telling you, clearly, she wants more, and you're acting like a thickheaded moron. You're playing with fire, if you want my opinion. But you've always been weird with women. You ever gonna settle down, man?"

"Sure. Someday. When the right woman says yes, I guess." *If* the right woman says yes, he had thought. And was Yvonne even the right woman? What did the right woman even mean? It sounded like something his mother would say. But he knew there was no such thing as the right women.

It was more like the woman he could live with.

He trusted Yvonne and she let him breathe, and that was all that mattered. That was no small feat for a woman.

Maybe after all this time, he and Yvonne were only meant to be friends.

He called Kadee a few times. No answer. He didn't leave a message. Pissed that she probably watched his number go across her phone screen and purposefully didn't answer, he stopped trying.

He told himself it was done, but by the next day when he hadn't heard from her, his thoughts were consumed with her. Kadee's fiery, passionate side infuriated him. But it must have also aroused him, because he spent the day at the office trying his hardest not to think about her and to keep himself from having a full-blown erection. He had to lock himself in the bathroom and jerk off twice that morning. Images of leaving work, going to her apartment, pulling her hair back and ripping her clothes off monopolized his thoughts all day.

He had to have her at least one more time.

God damn it!

Somehow, he made it through the afternoon without blasting another load at work. When he got home, he relieved himself, immediately. The desire for Kadee consumed him. He called her, again. She still hadn't called back. The need for her felt urgent. Obsessive. He must be nuts.

Damn it!

He distracted himself, went on Match.com, looked at some of the profiles of attractive women. Most of them looked like Kadee, dark hair, green eyes, tall and lanky, with curves. Every woman resembled Kadee. His mind felt jumbled.

Pornography would work better as a Kadee diversion, he decided. But as he watched, he saw Kadee's *bunk-bunk* hips, slim waist and trim bush in all of those women, too. His dick filled, *again*; he relieved himself, *again*. What on earth was wrong with him? He was furious and aroused and confused.

To make matters worse, Mother called.

Of course.

With her typical omniscient timing, she knew now was an opportune time to harass him. In her mellifluous voice, she explained that she had a new woman to fix him up with: Jennifer Papers. A daughter of a doctor friend. He knew who she was. Jennifer Papers had wide hips and the largest nose he had ever seen. It was one of those noses that was so huge it looked like part of a Halloween costume. Like a witch's, it stretched down toward her upper lip with a repulsive hook at the tip. All it needed was a ghastly wart on the side.

"Mother. Please. I'm not interested." He tried.

But Mother insisted and insisted, relentless as always.

"Fine. One date." He said, trying to contain his exacerbation.

Then she started on the whole Kadee debacle and how he best break it off. "Clearly the woman is in love with you.

Alas. Poor dear. Who wouldn't be? But since it's not going anywhere, the right thing to do is end it. I've always raised you to be honorable. Besides, we both know she's a whore. Listen to mother."

"Yes. Yes. Of course, you're right, Mother. You're always right, *Mother*."

"Does Mother hear contempt in your voice? Please tell me you aren't mocking Mother."

"Of course not." He looked at her picture on his nightstand, slammed it face down.

He hated her.

As soon as they hung up, he put a few of her other pictures face down.

But then a few minutes later, he picked up the picture on his nightstand and placed it in an upright position. "Sorry, mother." He said it to the picture as though Mother could see. He was a nut job. Mother could do that to a person: Make herself seem so omnipotent, she could control another's behavior even when she wasn't there.

He took a long, scalding shower. The entire bathroom filled with steam.

A little while later, Kadee called back.

Finally.

He explained the confusion that the woman was his mother. He had not told his mother that they had been dating, which is why he introduced her as a friend.

By the time they had hashed things out, the evening had ticked its way to ten o'clock. He took a chance by asking her to come over and stay the night. Surprisingly, she agreed.

That evening, he lay wrapped around Kadee as if his life depended on it.

In the middle of the night the kids voices jarred him awake. "Yo, Donovan, I heard you tongue-kissed your mother. Is it true, Noah dear? Did you kiss yo mama? Huh, did you? You did, didn't you? Noah and Belle sitting in a tree K-I-S-S-I-N-G."

"What is it?" Kadee perched up on her side. "You were mumbling something and sounded upset. Another nightmare?"

"Yeah."

"Tell me about it. It will help. I promise."

"No, it won't." He pulled away from her, scrunched up in the fetal position all the way at the edge of the bed.

She touched his back. "I'm here if you need me."

"Thanks."

Within a few minutes, he heard the rhythm of her breathing change. She fell asleep.

But Noah lay awake staring vacantly into the shadows. The memories always haunted him, but for some reason they seemed to be coming more frequently.

Mother had told him the truth one day. He wished she wouldn't have.

Some secrets were meant to be kept hidden. If they remained buried, then they weren't really true. Some secrets should never be shared.

After they moved to New York City, things got better. Mother made new friends; he went to a new school, all new kids, a place where no one knew about his past. He excelled in his classes and had friends. No more teasing him about Mother and the berries. Mother still came into his bed that first year, but then she met a new man, Pierre. Nothing overly serious, she had told Noah. But her bedroom visits stopped after that. Noah hated Pierre. He missed Mother's visits. He felt gross thinking that he missed her sleeping with him, so he did his best to block it out.

He missed his father, too, and Noah still believed whatever it was that happened was his fault. No matter how he looked at it, before his father died, his father had planned to leave Mother because of Noah — and take Noah with him. Noah was to blame. He broke the marriage apart and probably killed his father by breaking his heart.

If Mother did poison his father with the berries, then that was even more his fault, because she probably did it so his father wouldn't take him away. She had said, "No one will ever take you from me. Don't worry. I will make sure of it. Not even your father. Understand? Mother loves you more than anything."

Two days later, his father died on the floor of the kitchen.

Eventually, Mother told him the truth about the berries. It was worse than he had imagined.

Chapter 16

Summer rolled in and with that came thick, sticky, sultry city air. The burgeoning possibility of being in a relationship with Yvonne turned full bloom that summer. And Noah's Kadee-Yvonne conundrum turned from a dilemma into a web of duplicity.

Yvonne wanted to spend more time with him. Never demanding like Mother or Kadee, but her desire was there, and she clearly articulated her wants one June afternoon at lunch.

Noah spilled the "I want to marry you" statement, again. He said it not expecting anything in return. Yvonne looked at him, welling eyes, like she might shed a tear. Yvonne almost never cried. And he saw the love in those baby blues. He worried that she would say yes. He wanted her to say she wanted to marry him, even though he wasn't ready to *actually* marry her. More, he wanted a commitment from her, some confirmation that there was security in their future.

Through those watery eyes, Yvonne said, "I love you, Noah." He looked at her with a fullness in his heart. An unfamiliar feeling stirred within him: vulnerability. He grabbed her, squeezed her tight. "I never thought I'd hear you say those words."

"I know. I'm sorry it took me so long. I do love you, handsome. I want us to spend more time together. I'm ready."

"I want to marry you." He said it again, almost shocking himself with the veracity of his intention.

"Oh, handsome, you're such a sweetie. You really are." Then she gave him a playful shove, meaning, I'm not ready to go there, yet. You haven't earned fiancé status, yet, Noah Donovan. In that moment, he saw the ponytailed, bespectacled girl, tapping her toes, nostrils flaring, standing outside his apartment door that day back in medical school when he blew it with her by being a jerk after they had had sex.

Finally, she had moved past that.

Hallelujah.

"Let's have dinner tonight. Maybe catch a movie."

He gulped, said, "Plans with Mother tonight. How bout tomorrow?"

"OK. Tomorrow's good." She blinked a bunch of times.

"You're upset."

"No. Why would you say that?"

"You're doing the quick blinks. I know you're thinking something you don't want to say."

She blushed. "I guess, I worry about your relationship with your mother sometimes. She really has control over you.

And… if things progress with us, I worry that she will try to interfere."

"She won't. I promise." He pulled her close for a hug. "OK."

"OK."

Worse, the plans weren't with Mother. They were with Kadee.

After Noah left Yvonne's office, he went straight to Kadee's place.

Some afternoon's he would stop by, have sex with her, then quickly leave. In his mind, he pretended that he was a stranger, entering Kadee's apartment without her permission, ravaging and exploiting her sexually. A few times, he ripped her panties right off her. And she let him. Man, did that arouse him. In fact, the rough sex and Kadee's wild abandon when he posed as a stranger turned him on so much, he almost couldn't stop thinking about it. It was a role play he always fantasized about. And Kadee indulged him.

This new development with Yvonne was unexpected. He knew he had to break it off with Kadee, but he wasn't sure he could. He had tried a few times, but could not bring himself to end it. Meanwhile, he could tell Kadee wanted more of a commitment from him. Her needs were strangling him. The more she wanted, the more he pulled away emotionally. But that didn't stop him from seeing her.

Well, she could end it, too, he'd tell himself. *If she's so discontent, why the fuck doesn't she end it? Why is the onus on me? Kadee has free will.*

He could not end it, but he wished she would.

Maybe.

Every time he felt Kadee pull back a little, he panicked.

Before he left Kadee's that afternoon, she had said, "We're hanging out tonight. Right?"

They had made the evening plans the previous day. Before Yvonne dropped the "I love you" in his lap.

"Yeah. Just come over around 7:30. We'll order in."

"You don't want to go out. My favorite local band is playing downtown."

"Not tonight. Long week. I want to be low key."

She looked disappointed. Surely, because he wasn't meeting her needs. But she acquiesced with an, "OK." In fact, Kadee had become increasingly compliant and easy to control. Her weakness turned him off, but the power he felt over her gave him an adrenalin rush like he had never experienced before. That turned him on.

Kadee slept over that night.

The next morning turned into an absolute fiasco.

Noah lay in bed with Kadee, both half dozing. At 10:30 a.m., the *brrring* of the phone startled him. He took a heavy breath as he grabbed the phone.

Yvonne.

Shit.

"I need to grab this. Be right back."

Kadee looked wary. "OK."

He went into the living room and shut the bedroom door.

"Hey."

"Why are you whispering, handsome?"

"Oh, am I whispering? I was sleeping. Just groggy. How's your morning?"

"Would be better if you were here. Come over. I'll make you breakfast."

"I– I– uh, how bout in an hour?"

"Oh. You're busy now. My apologies. Silly me to ask so spontaneously."

He could hear the deflation in her voice.

"No. It's not silly at all, beautiful. I'll come now and take care of morning errands afterward. I'd love breakfast." Perspiration accumulated in his armpits and behind his neck.

"Wonderful. I'll start breakfast now. How does whole-wheat pancakes sound?"

"Delicious. Be there soon."

"Ta ta."

"Bye."

Back in the bedroom, Kadee sat up in the bed, a cagey expression still on her face.

"Who was it?" She said with a bite, starting a morning wrangle.

He diverted eye contact. "My mother."

"But it wasn't your mother's time to call. That wasn't like her." One eye squinted, lips scrunched up at the corners.

What did Kadee want? He had already answered her. He tried, again. "I said it was Mother, Kadee. Jeez. You're being too needy. Waaay too needy. I hate when you start this shit." He threw his hands up in the hair, pretending to look through his paperwork on his desk, so he wouldn't have to look at her.

Then came the lie: "I have to go out for a minute. My mother needs my help with something."

"I'll come with you."

"No. Wait here if you want. I won't be gone long."

"Fine." Kadee plopped back into his bed, flipped the television on.

"I'll be back soon."

He left for Yvonne's.

A disaster. He had to leave Kadee in his apartment. He had no other choice. With that expression of distrust on her face, she would have known he was up to something if he asked her to leave. Now he had to make sure he didn't stay at Yvonne's too long.

He had to break it off with Kadee.

Tomorrow.

The sweet aroma of pancakes and syrup filled his nose as soon as Yvonne opened her apartment door.

Her eyes lit up as soon as she saw him, blue as the clearest sky.

"Hi, beautiful."

"Oh, I like when you say that, handsome." She batted her eyelashes. A long kiss exchanged as soon as the door closed.

Yvonne broke the embrace. "Come sit. It's ready. Coffee to start?"

"Sure."

"Here. Two drip drops of milk, just the way you like it."

Yvonne warmed the pancakes. "So, my friend is having a party tonight on her roof deck. I thought it would be nice to go there instead of the movies. It's such a lovely morning. I bet the evening will be delightful. Won't it be nice to be outside? The summer isn't going to last forever." She put two plates down on the table. "Here you go, handsome." She smiled at him, adoringly.

"Which friend. Someone I know?"

"Oh, I don't think so. It's a friend from my yoga class."

"So, it's on the Upper Eastside?"

"Yes, she lives a few blocks from here."

Noah ate a few bites of pancake.

"Handsome, you're sweating. Do you want me to turn up the air conditioning?"

"That would be great. It's a hot morning."

"It is. But you know me. I like these warm days… so, how about the party?"

"Not tonight. It's not that I don't want to meet your friend and the party sounds fun." He took her hand, gave her an intense look, said, "I just want to spend some time alone with you tonight."

She smiled at him. "Of course. That sounds even better."

"But I am going to have to leave after we finish here. I have errands to run and I'm meeting J.C. to work on the research proposal."

"How's that going?"

"It's a lot of work. But it's moving along. You know how it is. So much detail."

"Yes. I do know. I really do. Listen. Tonight there is something I want to tell you. Something I need you to know before we go any further."

"What is it? Something I should be concerned about?"

"Oh, no. It's nothing bad about us. It's something about me. Something very personal that I never told you before. I have always wanted to tell you, but the time never really felt right. But it does now."

"Tell me now. I'll be preoccupied all day."

"Oh, I don't want to bring it up when you're pressed for time."

His brow furrowed.

"It's nothing, handsome. Sorry I even said anything before tonight." She kissed his lips. "It's nothing, really. Love you."

I am a bastard.

I will break it off with Kadee, today.

"Love you too, beautiful."

Noah walked back home with determined steps. Yvonne had said "before we go any further" and "love you." And she said it first this time. Breaking it off with Kadee was a must. He had to do it. She would definitely flip out. Women do that. It was to be expected. He'd allow her some leeway with the histrionics. Breakups were shitty for the dumpee.

With every step away from Yvonne's place, his resolve dwindled. Kadee and those *bunk-bunk* hips waited at his place.

You weak, pathetic son-of-a-bitch.
You will do this.
Will.

The apartment reeked of a... *what*... a cigarette? He smelled the foul odor; nearly choked as soon as he opened his door.

Kadee didn't smoke. Apprehensive, he made his way into the bedroom.

He discovered a mess with Kadee in the center of it. She sat on the wood floor straddling a smattering of cigarette ashes, photographs face down, a plastic container, panties. *Are they hers? What is she doing?* He scanned the floor, looked at Kadee, furious and confused.

She leapt up, screamed, "What the fuck is this shit, Noah?" She held up a computer memory stick.

What on earth was this crazy bitch up to? Those green eyes blazed at him, reaching out to burn him with flames.

"You tell me! What the fuck is this shit? You went through my things! And what is this?" He pointed at the container. Her container, he assumed. It wasn't his.

"It's your stuff!" she hollered, like a raging lunatic. "Why don't you tell me what *this* is?" She held another computer memory stick.

"I have no idea what *that* is, Kadee!"

Then she went on some ridiculous tirade about him keeping trophies of his conquests. She held up a pair of her own panties and acted like they weren't familiar to her. He hadn't the faintest idea what her problem was, but he was God damn furious.

She screamed, "Tell me the truth. Tell me the fucking truth already. You owe me that much for my porn movie."

He looked at her like she was nuts. "Porn? What the hell are you talking about?"

Controlling, suffocating whore was fabricating some new drama.

A memory stick banged him in the head.

That was it. She was throwing things at him. And what was she doing with those memories sticks, anyway. There were a few on the floor. What was on them?

"OK, that's it, Kadee. I think you should leave. I want you to leave." He gave her a severe look.

Suddenly, that fierce demeanor turned defeated and deflated. Her voice small, "You're throwing me out?"

Psycho bitch. Now she's acting all small and meek, trying to reel me back in after her dramatic freak out. No way.

She did this. She handed him his out on a silver platter.

"I'm asking you to leave," he said, restraining his anger.

Now Kadee's eyes welled.

Total psycho.

"So you're breaking up with me"

"I didn't say that. I don't know. I just want you to leave right now. We can talk about it later or tomorrow."

Why did you say that? Let her go. It was fun while it lasted. Say bye-bye.

"You're breaking up with me. Just say it."

"We can talk later."

He wanted to grab her and kiss her.

He hated her.

"Just say it!"

"Fine." He crossed his arms, glared right into those fiery green eyes.

"'Fine' what? Say it!"

"Fine. I'm breaking up with you!"

It was out.

Finally. She made him say it. He loved her for it. He hated her for it.

See, you got what you wanted, Kadee with a D.

Bitch.

She threw all that stuff scattered on the floor back into that plastic container. Who knows where she got that thing from. Still confused about what exactly inspired the fight, he watched her gather her stuff. Then, the psycho bitch threw a book at him.

"Ow! What the fuck!"

She smirked.

Maybe she enjoyed this.

He walked her to the door, thought about slapping her, but didn't. He mumbled, "I'll see you."

"God, I hope not." She shot daggers with her eyes. He watched her amble down the hall.

Finally, he ended it.

She was gone.

Hip hip hooray.

Chapter 17

Gone and forgotten were not the same.

Not even close

Within a few hours of Kadee's theatrical departure, he could not get the woman out of his head.

He abhorred her. Detested her neediness, her hyper-emotionality, and the scene she made was inexcusable. Yet, thoughts of her invaded his mind.

He went to the office to catch up on paperwork, trying to distract himself.

He needed to stay away from Kadee.

He would.

But no matter how many files he perused, the images of Kadee would not fade.

The sex was good, sure, but he was a forty-year-old man looking to settle down with another woman, a woman he had loved for years. What the hell? Maybe he needed a few days. But his stomach felt funny, and he could not chill out.

The phone mocked him every time he looked at the screen expecting a text from Kadee.

Ugh!

The pool seemed like the only place he would get any peace. With that, he headed over to the gym to swim laps. Being enveloped by water always calmed him. He used to swim for hours when he was a kid. Mother didn't swim. God forbid she messed her meticulously set hair. Water was the ideal place to get away from her. Far away.

The pool was empty except for a lone swimmer in the fast lane. A slight woman wearing a bright blue bathing cap swam a fast stroke. The smell of the chlorine and the swoosh of the water soothed him.

He jumped in, submerging his head. The way his body felt suspended in the water made him feel weightless, like his physical body no longer existed. No one could find him in that pool because he was nothing but his thoughts.

He let his body sink to the bottom of the pool, stayed under for as long as he could and watched the bubbles from his nose rise to the surface. The suffocation started, his chest hurt. He came up, choking for air.

He did it again.

The lifeguard peered over the side of the pool's edge, gave him an uneasy glare.

He waved his hand high above the water at her, nodded. She recognized he was alright, went back to her seat. She had long dark hair, like Yvonne and Kadee.

He shook his head, jettisoned the image of the women messing with his life. He let himself float on the surface, weightless in the water. He took in the peace. Then just when he felt he could let sleep take him to a watery end, he flipped over and dug in. His arms ripped through the water. With each stroke he felt clearer, calmer, more in control. Thoughts of Kadee disappeared. The ability to vanquish the images of her left him feeling powerful; with each rip through that water he felt more in command of his environment.

It was done.

That was a good thing.

Bye-bye Kadee. It was fun while it lasted.

When he finished his laps, he felt relaxed as he slowly glided to the ladder. But as soon as he got out of the water, he thought *I love Kadee.*

His eyes bugged out at the realization.

Bitch.

I do NOT love her.

The thought trespassed on his peace. He did not like that.

He definitely didn't love her. Rather, he decided, she had made him her victim. Exactly what he worried about and suspected when he met her that day in line at the coffee shop, Kadee turned out to be the type of woman who consumed men, then tossed them out in chewed up pieces.

Whore.

Any woman who would exploit her sexuality to get a man to do what she wanted was a whore. Mother warned him about this type of woman. Mother knew this from personal experience. How many men had he witnessed Mother manipulate? Too many to count.

Mother was a whore, too.

That thought twisted his stomach into a knot. *Sorry, Mother.* Mother could do that to a person: Make someone apologize profusely for a private thought.

But Mother is benevolent. His inner voice tried to cancel out *Mother is a whore.*

Mother was a victim.

Guilt: a wasted emotion. But when it came to Mother, that wasted emotion festered beneath the surface and led him to do things he didn't want to do. Such as listen and obey Mother like he was still that needy, dependant little boy.

Mother told him the truth about his father. He wished she hadn't. But Mother never truly considered what was good for him — or anyone for that matter. She would say that everything she did was for him.

"Everything mother does is for you, Noah dear." She repeated that sentence frequently.

Unfortunately, that was a big fat load of crap. He believed her when he was a child, but by the time he reached high school, he knew Mother only did what was good for *her*. Anything that appeared to be a munificent gesture toward him ended up being a crafty subterfuge to get *him* to do what *she* wanted.

And man was she good at *that*.

Knowing what happened to her made it hard to stand up for himself. She preyed on weakness and could sniff it with the shrewdness of the best-trained hound dog.

Father had tried to poison mother with those poisonous berries, the ones Max had found in the jar. On his eleventh birthday, his mother graced him with the truth. Father knew she would never give up Noah, so he got his hands on poisonous berries, Belladonna. His father had planned to poison Mother that morning. "He thought he had it all figured out. But Mother was smarter," she had told Noah the day she spilled the ugly story.

Mother found some information on Belladonna in his briefcase, then a few mornings later, his father got up early and made her breakfast. She saw him putting the berries in her food, but father didn't know mother saw. Mother had these delicate little footsteps. His father must have forgotten that and got careless, because Mother witnessed him crushing loads of berries and putting them in her cereal bowl.

Father and Mother were barely speaking at this point. Mother knew he was up to something. She couldn't trust him, so she switched their cereal bowls when he got up to get orange juice. She wasn't quite sure what was going to happen.

Then, his father died from the poison. Mother felt horrible, but she feared for her life. "Your father was a powerful man," she had told Noah that day. "He wouldn't have stopped until he killed me. Please understand. I had no choice. Mother is sickened by the whole thing. We must never discuss this again. Mother is only telling you because she felt you had a right to know the truth about who your father was."

Tears had rolled down Noah's cheeks as his mother relayed these terrible details. Noah believed her. Every word.

He never told anyone, and no one ever found out the truth. No one he knew in New York even knew about the rumors. He carried that secret around with him, everyday, a ponderous weight pushing heavily on a young child. It was always sort of there, pulling him down, even though he tried his best not to think about it at all. And it only got heavier as he grew.

Mother was so cunning, though. It took him a long time to realize that about Mother. Sometime in his late teens, he began to recognize her ability to control him and everyone else. Occasionally, he wondered if that story was really the truth. He didn't know which was worse, the story Mother told, or believing that Mother plotted and planned to poison his father so as not to lose custody of him. Neither story constructed a past he wanted to be a part of. Either way, his father's death was his fault. Deep down, that secret, along with the memories of Mother coming into his bed, tormented him.

Chapter 18

Before he left for Yvonne's, Kadee called a few times. He watched her number scroll across his cell phone screen. He wanted to pick up, but didn't. He needed a Kadee detox, he had decided.

He felt triumphant when he saw her number pop up, though — and pop up more than once. Regardless, if he had been her conquest, he was the one in control now. She was his subordinate, not the other way around.

Bitch.

The pull to call her was stronger than he wanted to admit to himself, though. He shut his phone off, then left for Yvonne's in a rush, trying to run away from the thoughts about Kadee that plagued him.

"Hi, handsome." Yvonne greeted him at the door. Those dazzling baby blues lit up her face.

"Hey." He gave her a tight hug. "Let's order in tonight. Maybe watch a movie or something low key."

"OK. How about the Italian place around the corner?" She produced a menu from her drawer.

"Sounds good. You order. I'll have whatever you decide."

"Oh no. I'm not falling into that trap. You can make your own decisions." She shoved an elbow into his side and gave him a knowing smile.

"Ha! Alright. I'll have the meat ravioli."

"That sounds good. I'm going to get that, too."

Yvonne ordered the food in the kitchen. Noah went into her living room, plopped into her beige couch. Yvonne's living room really needed some color. All of the furniture was a boring beige, a monotonous sea of blah. Even the art work on the wall held no vibrancy. In fact, her bedroom was blah, too: beige sheets, brown comforter, dark wood furniture, colorless adornments. Just one red throw pillow, meager enthusiasm on an otherwise tedious palate, stood out as the exception. Yvonne, she had been hauling that red pillow around with her since medical school. Yvonne had some weird attachment to it. She said she kept it as a memento from that time in her life. Strings hung from the edges and had a musty smell. She also had a framed poster of Tweety Bird on her wall. Yvonne loved Tweety Bird. "The way he controls Sylvester cracks me up," she would say. "Besides, he's adorable."

As soon as Yvonne came into the living room, he asked, "So what is it that you wanted to tell me?"

Her face grew long.

"What?"

She sat down on the couch next to him. Their knees touched. She folded her hands in her lap.

"I feel I've been dishonest."

Noah's brow furrowed. "Oh?"

"Yes. And I apologize."

"OK?"

"See. You had shared with me what happened when your mother used to crawl into bed with you, and we discussed how it was inappropriate."

He gazed into his lap. "Yeah."

"Well, I wanted to tell you then, but I just couldn't. I don't even know why. It's always been so hard for me to trust people. But I want you to know all of me. I want to trust you."

He put his hand on her leg. "And you can."

"I know that now, handsome. You have been so patient with me. Something similar happened to me with my uncle when I was a girl. My father's brother. He touched me. And he touched my brother, James, too. And… well, I wanted to tell my parents. But he made me promise not to. He said if we told, he would move from touching us to penetration. I was frightened. So I said nothing. It continued on and off even through high school." A tear rolled down Yvonne's cheek.

Noah wiped it from her face. "It's OK." He gave her a warm look.

"It's not, though. You see, I think James killed himself after he told his girlfriend, Bettina, the truth, and she broke up with him. I told him to tell Bettina. I told him to tell her, even though I knew it wasn't the right thing to do. You see, James and I were so close. And when Bettina started to come around, he spent a lot less time with me. So I told him to tell her so she'd break up with him. And she did. Then James killed himself. I'm a horrible person for doing that." Tears streamed down Yvonne's face.

He took her head and rested it on his shoulder, rubbed her head. "It's OK. Come on. You were only a kid. You just did what kids do. It wasn't your fault. Isn't that what you would tell me?"

She nodded yes, while her head rested on him.

He squeezed her petite frame as tight as he could. "It's OK."

"Do you still love me?" She looked up at him with big doe eyes, sniffled.

"Of course."

"Say it."

"I love you, Yvonne."

"Love you, too." She hugged him tight.

They stayed like that, no more words, until the food arrived.

When Noah got up to get the food, Yvonne looked at him, "I'm glad I told you. I really felt that you deserved to know. But I don't want to talk about it anymore. I needed to tell you and that's all. OK?"

"You got it, beautiful."

Noah spent the night with Yvonne. In the morning, he stared at the ceiling. Restlessness festered. He didn't understand why. She had shared that intimate secret with him, and he had felt close to her when she told him. But by morning, he felt like he wanted to run out. He knew he had to stay for a while, so he untangled himself from her embrace, got up and made her breakfast.

Thankfully, they both had to leave for work soon after. She held him tight before they parted ways. "Come back tonight," she looked so vulnerable when she asked.

"Sounds good, beautiful." But he felt uneasy about the whole thing, like he needed space from her. But he could not screw this up, again. "I'm working late, but I'll come by afterward."

"Great, handsome. Ta, ta," she said, a big smile covered her face. She kissed him once more before he walked out.

He went home, showered, prepared to head over to the office. When he looked for some notes he had written down for a journal article he was working on, he found a few framed pictures of mother on his desk, one with a big black **X** across her face and **Love Mother** in big red letters across the bottom.

Whaaat?

He stared at it in disbelief. Kadee found pictures of Mother and crossed her out of one of them? What the hell.

Crazy bitch.

He only had patients until two o'clock that day. As soon as he was done, he ran to Kadee's and banged on her door like a maniac. His fury over her hysteria the previous morning stewed to an unbearable point. By the middle of the afternoon, he had decided he had to know why she went through his things and where she got that container and the pictures of Mother. He wanted to know what went on while he had left her — trusted her, in his apartment, alone, the previous day.

"Kadee, open up. I know you're there." *Bang. Bang. Bang.*

He jiggled the door knob, ready to kick the door in if he had to. He could see the shadow of her feet through the bottom crack of the door frame. "Open up, Kadee." He hollered, furious and frenetic.

While he banged on that door, he felt himself becoming erect, which made him more irate and more desperate.

In a lull from his banging frenzy, he heard the *whish whish* of her feet move away from the door, then come back, hovering right in front of it. He made his eyes huge, put them right up to the peephole. He felt positive she was looking at him through the hole. In a steady voice, he attempted to persuade her. "I know you're there. I can hear you. Please… Please… open up. Please, Deedee. I'm sorry."

Kadee opened the door.

He flew in, paced. "Where did those pictures of Mother come from? Where did you get them?"

"There're yours. I found them under your desk where you were hiding them along with the other things."

"There're not mine. Did you cross off Mother's face?" He paced faster.

"I found them under your desk. Listen, I shouldn't have been under there. I shouldn't have gone through your things. It was wrong of me. But those videos – "

"There're not mine!"

"Well, whose are they, then? They were under your desk. They aren't mine!" She hollered and her face turned bright red.

"And you're right. You shouldn't have gone through my things."

"I apologize. I was out of line. I wish you would have just been honest with me. I didn't know what was going on with you, with us. It was driving me crazy. Did you know that? You're driving me crazy!"

"*You're* driving *me* crazy!"

Their eyes locked. Her eyes wide, an expression of innocent exasperation, and he wanted her. He wanted her fiercely, desperately, violently. In a moment of reckless desire, he pulled her close, grabbed her face, kissed her furiously. Her lips were warm and she pressed those *bunk-bunk* hips against him. He pushed her up against the wall, ripped the neck of her T-shirt right in half. She stood naked except for her panties. He wanted her exposed.

He tore the panties off her, shoved her down on the couch, penetrated her naked body with his eyes. God, she was gorgeous. He never wanted a woman so completely, so wildly. An invisible magnet pulled him. He resisted, let her lay naked while he stood back and admired her.

Wide eyes, a look of unease, she tried to cover her body with a blanket. He stopped her, took the blanket out of her hand, leaving her with nothing to cover herself. She was his in that moment. A sudden thought of *I love her*, trespassed in his mind. Her green eyes lured him with an almost naïve consternation, like she didn't know what he was doing or what he wanted.

He removed his pants and entered her. Kadee abandoned herself completely to him; let him take her exactly the way he wanted, carelessly, furiously, totally. He came hard and fast, ejaculating on Kadee's long, thin neck. The semen lay near her throat, evidence of his possession of her seconds earlier. When she went to wipe it off, he took her hand away, made her keep it there until he cleaned himself off first.

As she lay there, shamed, his glory slipping around her glorious neck, he still felt aroused and briefly debated taking her again.

Then, she pulled him down to lay with her, which disturbed the overpowering grip she had had on him. Suddenly, his thoughts cleared. He needed to leave her and that sexual power she had. She controlled him, made him want her impetuously and recklessly, even violently. "I have to go."

A look of shock splayed across Kadee's face. "What?" She wiped the semen off her neck and grabbed the nearest blanket to cover her body.

"Sorry. I have patients. I'll call you later."

Kadee's eyes welled. A dramatic display of emotions loomed. It strangled him.

"What?" she asked again. "C'mon. Stay for a little while."

She asked him to stay even though he told her he had to leave.

"Don't be needy. I have to go." He moved toward the door.

With a look of horror, Kadee shoved him toward the door, then into the hallway. She yelled into the corridor loud enough for anyone within a block radius to hear. "You fucking bastard, don't call me later. Don't call me ever."

A few more F-words and an "I hate you" spewed out of her mouth, echoing against the walls of her hallway until he finally exited her building.

I hate you, too, Kadee with a D.

Problem was, he only hated her because he loved her. The more detached and aggressive the sexual relationship became, the more he hated her. She drove him to want her desperately and he abhorred her for it. *The woman is evil. Evil. Evil. Evil!* He abhorred her. And adored her. He couldn't stay away from her.

He still didn't know where Kadee got the pictures of Mother. He wondered if Mother hadn't put them there. Mother was capable of just about anything. But, he thought, crossing out a photo of herself, seemed far- fetched even for her.

After leaving Kadee's, he went home and searched under his desk, on top of his desk, and went through the drawers to see if he could figure out where that container and the photos came from. Nothing. He couldn't trust that Kadee was telling the truth. She probably planted it there to manipulate him. But where would she get the pictures. Maybe he would ask Mother.

Mother called a little while later, rambling on about something or other. His mind already felt restless, and Mother on a tangent about some inconsequential bullshit wasn't focusing his attention. "Noah, dear. Are you listening to me?"

"Yes. Of course mother. I always listen to you." He rolled his eyes. The woman exhausted him.

Women exhausted him.

He went to Yvonne's around 8:30 p.m., even though he didn't want to. Kadee called and texted, he watched her number pop up over and over. She wasn't even giving him a chance to call back, not that he had any intention to. The more she called, the longer he would make her wait for a return call. But the calls distracted him. He kept seeing her naked body on her couch. The images aroused him.

Bitch.

Being with Yvonne was better than he thought. Though he still felt a bit restless all night. Conversations with Yvonne always engaged him, but for some reason he felt bored that night. She kept asking, "Is everything alright, handsome?"

"Of course, beautiful." He responded. For the most part, everything was alright. He didn't even know why he felt uneasy. Here he was with Yvonne Tracy, the girl he had loved his entire adult life, the only girl he ever loved. Finally, he was with her. They were together. And suddenly, nothing felt the way he thought it should.

Later, while Yvonne slept soundly, Noah stared at her white, perfectly painted ceiling. His sleeplessness was Kadee's fault. If she would stop calling and tempting him with her persuasive sexuality, he would be able to lighten up and settle in with Yvonne. If Kadee messed this up for him, he'd kill her.

Chapter 19

I need to stay away from Kadee. I want to marry Yvonne. I will stay away from Kadee. I will stay away from Kadee. I am writing this to hold myself accountable. Noah wrote in his journal.

It had been almost a year since he last wrote in his journal. His confusion led him to start marking up those pages with his inner thoughts. Sometimes when he wrote, his feelings would become clearer. The school counselor he saw while in college had recommended this to him. He had gone for visits for almost a year.

Mother drove him nuts, more nuts than usual, when he moved out of their apartment and into the college dorms his freshman year. He wanted an objective person to talk to. It didn't change anything. Mother was Mother. But it was helpful to have a space to talk where Mother couldn't intrude. That was not a small thing. Mother not having access to any aspect of his life was not a small thing at all.

Knowing he saw a counselor drove mother a little batty, too. Mother didn't like not being privy to every part of him. In fact, he stayed with the counselor longer than he needed to or wanted to as a dig to Mother. He felt particularly powerful when he had told her, "No. I don't want you to call him, and I'm not signing a consent."

Mother being Mother, she called Mr. Shearstone, his counselor. Using all of her magnificent charm, she attempted to wheedle him into speaking with her. "I'm sorry, Mrs. Donovan. Noah's an adult. Unless it's an emergency, I can't speak with you without Noah's consent. And he has not consented." His response to mother was the same every time she asked.

"Noah, dear, I need you to sign that consent."

"No. This is something for me. Not this time."

Mother kept trying, though. At least she was consistent. If nothing else, he could always depend on mother's consistency. She called about once every other week, trying to get Shearstone to talk to no avail.

He had started writing in the journal again the previous week. He wanted to end it with Kadee, propose for real to Yvonne. It was what he thought he wanted, but his thoughts did not match his actions. As the visits to Kadee progressed, the sex became increasingly rough. It interfered with his plans with Yvonne, too. That was the worst part. The absorption with Kadee and her *bunk-bunk* hips clouded his judgment about Yvonne. He feared an impending disaster.

So he wrote in the journal.

You can only hate someone who you first loved, Noah wrote that evening. That was the truth. Sometimes he didn't write because the truth came out without his permission. Sometimes he didn't want to know the truth. He took that page, ripped it into tiny pieces and threw it in the trash. For good measure, he tossed the grinds from that morning's coffee on top of the shredded paper. If he didn't have to look at those words, they weren't real.

Chapter 20

"**Will you marry** me?" There he said it.

Hallelujah.

Two days after shredding his journal entry, he popped the question in Yvonne's office. He had been working up toward asking her and the question finally slipped out of his mouth. They faced each other, her baby blues gripping his attention. A history of emotion swirled between them. In that moment, he loved her more than ever. Yvonne was the last untainted woman in all of Manhattan, and he wanted to spend his life with her.

Finally, after two days of intense contemplation, he felt released from the untidy emotional entanglement with Kadee. He knew what he wanted: to marry the woman he always wanted to marry, Yvonne.

Hip hip hooray

Finally, Donovan, you got your shit together.

"Come on, Noah." She released a slight chuckle, tossed a small pillow from her couch at him. She tried to make light of the question. But her cheeks grew bright red. Yvonne flushed and he knew she wanted to say yes; she probably needed a minute to absorb what he had asked.

He felt the intensity between them.

Yvonne leaned her body against him, pulled him tight.

Here it comes; she's gonna say it. She's gonna say, yes. Yes, handsome.

Her body felt hot and he hugged her back. Then she said, "I'm sorry, Noah, but I have a session at 4:00. You have to go."

He felt pissed, but kissed her anyway. Women think that question is easy to ask. They can just take their time to answer, leaving a dude hanging from a string while they consider what *they* want.

"See you soon." She said.

"See you soon."

Now we're back on the see you soon crap?

Thank goodness he waited for her to pick out the ring.

Clearly, she wanted him to beg. He knew she wanted to say yes. With Yvonne, patience was apparently a must.

After work, he went over to Kadee's. She had texted and invited him over. In an impetuous moment, he wrote back, said he would be over around 7 p.m.. They ordered a pizza. Kadee went on about some intellectual disagreement she had had earlier that day with one of her fellow students. Noah enjoyed hearing her rant. Her intensity when it came to these sorts of esoteric philosophical matters entertained him. The vehemence of her position blazed. It was the same little character trait that she maintained with him in the bedroom, a type of untamed, reckless abandonment of self-consciousness. An enviable freedom he never had. It was undeniably attractive on Kadee.

He pushed the pizza box to the side, grabbed her mid-sentence and ripped another T-shirt of hers right down the middle. It felt so freeing to rip her shirt, and she seemed to enjoy the aggressiveness, which turned him on even more. She thrust her naked breasts into his chest and pulled him toward the couch and then down onto her body. Quickly, he took his jeans off, then entered her and pushed hard moving in synch with her bunk-bunk hips.

Once they finished as he lay on the couch next to Kadee, Noah felt dizzy, brought on by the breathlessness following the intense sexual experience. She curled up next to him. He knew she wanted him to stay. A real pain in the ass given his current situation of trying to stay the hell away from her.

"I have to go."

"I knew you were going to say that. I knew it. You're such a liar."

"I didn't lie."

"I asked you if things were going to change and you said yes. You said you would be more attentive and respectful. Not running out after sex is high up on that list. Just in case you didn't know."

"Kadee. Jeez. We hung out for a couple of hours. It's not like I came over, had sex with you and left. You are being needy. It's *you* that's doing this. Not me. When you're needy, it makes me feel like I need space. You need to back off."

Her eyes grew furious and he thought for sure she would stab him with a sharp object. "Get OUT!" She screamed. "Stop calling me. OUT." A determined pointer finger aimed at the front door. "I said OUT, you liar."

He stumbled to put his clothes on and get out of her apartment as fast as he could. That look in her eyes gave him chills, the look of insanity. It was the same look he saw on Mother the day his father died when he found Mother hovering over his father as he lay on the kitchen floor. He would never forget her eyes that day, a maniacal, panicked look. Seeing that look on Kadee made his hair stand on end. He wondered if she might kill him.

Chapter 21

"Yvonne Tracy, will you marry me."

Central Park, under the large oak tree near the zoo, Yvonne's favorite place in the park. That's where Noah tried the romantic approach. Down on one knee, a public display of his affection and commitment. Yvonne stood before him. With a wide smile and batting eyelashes, those baby blues welled.

"Yes, handsome. Yes! I want to marry you."

He stood up, embraced her. People passing by gazed over. Expressions of curiosity and adoration, nosy eyes scanned the scene, warm smiles, knowing glances, a few loud applauds. The people acted as if they had a personal invitation to participate in what should have been a very private moment.

Noah sweated. He hated the public demonstration. The inquisitive onlookers felt like a bunch of intrusive Mothers: Mother times one hundred. After asking Yvonne the previous day in the privacy of her apartment and getting the brush off — again, he decided she needed the fuss and excitement of a public proposal.

And it worked.

Hallelujah

Mid-September. The weather was an ideal mix of a warm sun and a cool breeze. Noah had brought Yvonne to the park under the guise of a picnic. Yvonne brought her favorite checkered blanket and egg salad sandwiches. Noah had a bottle of Champagne and two glasses in his backpack. He popped the cork, a *hissss* followed as bubbles dripped over the side. He poured two glasses. Then, he kissed Yvonne's lips. "To you finally saying yes." They clicked glasses, then sipped.

Yvonne beamed. He had never seen her skin glow with such radiance.

"This is the happiest day of my life. I'm sorry it's taken me so long. I've always loved you, Noah. I just love you so much it scares me. Sometimes it's easier to be with someone you love with a piece of your heart, instead of your entire heart. And, well... I love you completely. I had to wait and make sure you loved me as completely as I loved you. So I could trust this."

Looking at the honest vulnerability in her eyes terrified him. She did trust him and he wasn't worthy.

What was he doing?

"I have always loved you, too. I'm just not very good at it."

"You brought me to my favorite place, got down on one knee in front of everyone in the park as a testament of your love for me. That shows me that you're serious and willing to make the sacrifices necessary for a marriage to work." She kissed his lips.

Suddenly, he felt uneasy.

They sat on the checkered blanket, sipping Champagne. A barrage of wedding plans flooded out of Yvonne's mouth. They'd have a loft wedding. She already knew the perfect caterer. Then on to a honeymoon in Paris. Some other stuff that Noah stopped paying attention to. He hadn't given much thought passed the "I do," part.

Shit.

This just got real.

"What do you think, handsome?" Those baby blues glowed with excitement. They were gentle and welcoming, yet those baby blues felt like two claws gripping his throat.

"Sounds great." He said, trying to sound upbeat.

"Which part?"

"All of it."

"The first thing we need to do is get the ring. I know you said you didn't want to get it without my approval, that you wanted me to pick it out. And this makes sense. It really does. But I want *us* to pick it out. I want *us* to go together and pick it out together. It's no more me and you. It's *us*."

Noah felt a burst of perspiration, a hot flash.

"Handsome, you're sweating." She took a napkin, wiped the dots of sweat off his brow.

He moved her hand gently off of his head, took the napkin and wiped his own brow. "It's hot today."

"It's not that hot." She gave him a curious look. It felt penetrating. He suddenly wanted to scream *STOP IT.*

"Maybe you should have some blood work done. You're always hot. Could be your thyroid."

"I'm fine. Come on, I'm a doctor too. It's probably the Champagne." He put his arm around her slim back, pulled her close and hoped she would stop talking.

"Let's go look at rings today." She looked at her watch. "It's still early."

His stomach dropped.

Yvonne started packing the food up. "Come on."

He avoided her eyes as he helped her pack up the food and fold the blanket.

A few minutes later, Noah slid next to Yvonne in the back of a taxi on the way to buy an engagement ring. The car inched through the heavy traffic. Noah felt antsy. He held Yvonne's hand.

It was all happening too fast.

Pressure squeezed his chest.

"Beautiful, I'm not feeling so well." He looked at Yvonne with a forced pained expression.

"You don't look well, either. What is it?"

"My head. A migraine."

"You know you should really see someone about these migraines."

"I know."

"I apologize." She said to the taxi driver. "Can you turn around and drop us on 76th and Park, please."

The driver, a heavy set man with bushy eyebrows and thick fingers, nodded, turning left on Fifth Avenue to head north.

"I'll come back to your place with you. Take care of my handsome fiancé."

He put his arm around her shoulders.

Of course you will.

As soon as Yvonne and he entered his apartment, she hurried into his bedroom. Dragging his feet, he followed behind her. She turned down the sheets and patted the bed. "Come. Get in. I'll get your medicine." She unbuttoned his jeans, pulled them down, scooted his body back into the bed.

Noah got in.

The sounds of Yvonne fumbling in the medicine cabinet irritated the shit out of him. She went through his stuff. It felt intrusive.

Yvonne never acted that way. She was ever mindful of his need for space.

What the fuck?

An engagement and suddenly the woman owned him?

She came back in; migraine pill and a glass of water in hand, blue eyes with a concerned determination. He noticed the slightest nostril flair and he knew she was pissed about the ring.

He groaned, rubbed his temple. "Thanks, beautiful." He said in whisper. "I hope you're not upset about the ring. We'll go tomorrow."

"It's OK. I understand. I really do."

"You seem pissed."

"I'm disappointed. I'll get over it. Now go to sleep. I'll be in the other room calling my family to share our news."

He heard her humming softly as she went into the other room. She pulled the bedroom door, leaving it open a crack.

He grabbed the cheeked migraine pill from his mouth and stuck it under his mattress.

You are a total ass. If you screw this up and she leaves, you deserve it.

Kadee had sent a string of texts. She invited him over. He didn't respond, but while he lay in his bed recovering from his feigned headache, he could not stop thinking about her. It wasn't just her naked body with those sexy *bunk-bunk* hips, either. He thought about the way her green eyes lit up when she went off on some intellectual diatribe, that spark of subversive zeal she exuded. The way she dressed, slightly careless, shirts untucked and her jeans threadbare, unruly, untamed. Sometimes he enjoyed teasing her, pretending he disagreed with her position on some topic so she would get fired up and argue with him. Kadee was unafraid of emotions.

He could never be with Kadee long term; she wasn't the kind of women that could ever be trusted. He had enjoyed that way about her, though.

Bye-bye, Kadee. It was fun while it lasted.

It was over now. He would marry Yvonne. He only hoped she wouldn't turn into Mother and strangle the life out of him.

Her excitement made her overzealous.

That had to be it.

I love Yvonne. I love Yvonne. Yvonne will be my wife.

He remembered Yvonne's words: "Sometimes it's easier to be with someone you love with a piece of your heart instead of your entire heart."

No. No. He did NOT love Kadee.

He hated her.

He loved Yvonne.

Now he actually had a headache. He looked for the pill he had stuffed under the mattress, took the water and swallowed the pill in a thick gulp.

He heard Yvonne on the phone in the other room. "Oh yes, this is the happiest day of our lives. We are excited to begin this new chapter together."

The glare of the white ceiling hurt his head. He closed his eyes, desperate for sleep to take him. But it never did.

Thank goodness he took that pill, though, because an hour later, Yvonne, bright as a street lamp, came in. "We need to call your mother and share the good news."

"Ugh, beautiful. Not now. My head still hurts."

"I know it won't be an easy conversation. But we need to tell her eventually. The sooner we get it over with the better."

He was no longer a *he*. He was now part of a *we*.

"Scoot over," she plopped onto the bed next to him, handed him his cell phone.

He grabbed it. Although he had the screen locked, he worried Yvonne would see his texts. He hadn't erased Kadee's most recent stream of messages.

He needed to tell Kadee to stop calling him.

Or change his phone number.

He hit mother's number and gave Yvonne a heavy sigh.

"It's OK, handsome. I'm here. You can do this." She took his free hand, placed it in her lap.

Noah's chest felt like an elephant had sat on it. Mother was going to go ballistic. He hadn't even told her he was seeing Yvonne. Mother did not like secrets, unless she was the one keeping them.

"Hello, dear."

"Hello Mother."

"Did you call Jennifer?"

"No. I didn't. Mother there is something I want to tell you." He looked at Yvonne. She mouthed, *go ahead.*

He got off the bed, walked slowly back and forth in the bedroom.

"What is it?" Mother's voice poked at him.

"I have proposed to Yvonne. And she has said yes. I am going to marry her."

Yvonne mouthed, *we are getting married.*

"We– we are getting married… Mother."

Silence.

Mother being silent was not a good thing. Noah wiped his brow, beads of sweat accumulated.

Yvonne's eyelashes fluttered furiously as she observed his every move.

He felt boxed in, trapped like an animal in a small cage, surrounded by starving, circling predators.

The thought of fleeing his apartment ran through his mind. And he considered actually doing it. If he could run far enough away, maybe everyone would leave him the fuck alone.

"Mother, say something."

"You can't marry Yvonne," she huffed. "She's almost forty. She'll never be able to give us babies. And she's got that belly. She doesn't take care of her appearance. It's all downhill from here. Besides, she drones on and on and on… about nothing. She will bore you to tears. Then, when you decide to divorce her because she's fat, barren and boring, she will try to take all of *our* money. Now you must trust Mother on this. Your judgment is severely compromised when it comes to women."

"Mother, I love her." He looked over at Yvonne. "Don't you want me to be happy?"

"Of course, dear. That's all I ever wanted. That's why I'm trying to stop you from making the biggest mistake of your life."

What a load of crap. She didn't want him to be happy.

"I don't agree. I thought about my decision to propose for a long time before I did it."

"Really. That's interesting because I know you still have that girlfriend — I mean slut — Kadee."

He looked over at Yvonne, whose eyes were glued to him. Sweat marks developed under his armpits.

"That's not true."

"Oh. It is. Haven't you learned that you can't keep secrets from Mother?"

He had learned that. Yet, how could mother know about Kadee. Unless she…

"Let's meet for dinner, Mother, and discuss this. OK? I really want your approval, but I am going to do this with or without it."

His skin burned from fury. That container Kadee found with those pictures, did Mother have something to do with that? Mother had come into his apartment while he wasn't home and had done something… something malevolent and intrusive. Something malicious and devious even for Mother. It was the only thing that made sense. And now she knew about Kadee.

This was not a good thing. Mother with that sort of confidential information, confidential information which could ruin his future with Yvonne, was akin to Mother with a loaded pistol ready to fire whenever necessary.

He wanted to vomit.

Or maybe she made it all up and happened to be right. Mother could do that to a person: Make someone question anything they thought was true. Mother could know someone so well she would know what they were doing without any concrete evidence *and* know what they were going to do even before they did it. Either way, he needed to talk with Mother, convince her not to say anything.

"Let's have dinner tomorrow. OK. I want us to talk."

"Mother is busy tomorrow evening. Let me see if I can change my plans. I'll call you in the morning."

Click. She hung up.

"Bye, Mother." He said to a dial tone.

With heavy eyelids and a long face, he looked at Yvonne. He wanted to kill Mother. If anyone deserved to die, it was her. The woman was impossible.

"It went well, handsome. You had to know she'd give you a hard time. She's obsessed with you. Always has been. Give her time to let it sink in. She'll come around."

"Right."

"You set a boundary with her. I'm very proud of you. You told her you were going to do it with or without her blessing. I've never heard you stand up to her like that before. It's a good thing."

"Right."

"Listen. I never wanted to say this before, but your mother is sick. Her infatuation with you is unhealthy."

"She raised me all alone after my father died. It couldn't have been easy. I was all she ever had. I don't want to talk about this." *She killed him because of me*, he thought, then quickly, shoved the notion out of his mind. "I've told you before, I don't want to *ever* talk about my past."

"Handsome, I'm a psychiatrist. I know for a fact that talking about the past can heal deep wounds from childhood.

It will help. It really will. I talked to a therapist for a long time about what I told you happened to me. It helped. It would help you, too."

"No. It won't. Talking about bad shit makes it more real. Some secrets are meant to stay buried. Some things are too horrible to say out loud. Understand."

He had told Yvonne about Mother crawling into bed with him naked and rubbing against him, and that he blamed himself for his father's heart attack. But he never told her about the berries. He never told her that Mother killed his father. In fact, that secret stayed locked so tight, sometimes he pretended it never really happened.

"OK." Yvonne backed off. "OK. I don't agree. I think some day you should talk about it. I hope it won't affect our future together."

What the fuck? Now it's all about her and her future. I was violated by Mother and she's worried about her future — our future.

"I need to take a shower. I don't want to talk about this anymore."

"When you get out, let's talk about happy things. Like our wedding plans." She gave him a warm, loving smile.

"Yes. Let's do that."

He turned and rolled his eyes.

A half hour later, Noah got out of the shower. The sweet aroma of tomato sauce filled the apartment. Yvonne had cooked pasta in his kitchen. Her hair was pulled back in a ponytail, a white apron tied around her slim waist. She turned and smiled, aimed a long wooden spoon at his mouth, "Here. Taste this."

He licked the spoon. "Delicious."

I love her, he thought. He adored watching her cook. Yvonne had this meticulous way about her. She hovered over the dinner she prepared with a refined concentration, making sure everything was cooked to absolute perfection. He poured them both a glass of white wine, sat on a kitchen chair and watched her cook.

The shower seemed to clear his thoughts. He felt suffocated by the idea of marriage, not Yvonne. The idea that he would lose her over the Kadee business sent fear through his veins. If he didn't love her, he wouldn't be afraid of losing her. He did love her.

Later that night, curled up in his bed, they discussed wedding plans. Yvonne wanted a loft wedding. She wanted to get married in the spring; six months was long enough for them to plan the wedding. A honeymoon in Paris and, if time allowed, perhaps a few days in Italy or Spain, too. Noah's head spun, but he indulged her. That's what people did when they loved each other: listen and listen and listen some more, even when they wished the person they loved would shut the fuck up.

I am an awful person, he thought that night while Yvonne slept soundly, a small smile across her lips. He stared at the ceiling. She really loved him; she trusted him with her heart. And he loved her with his heart. But in his mind, he stabbed her over and over.

He would try harder to be the man she thought he was.

He wanted to be that man for her.

Chapter 22

The right thing and the easy thing are never the same thing.

The next day he couldn't stop thinking about Kadee. The ruminations started as soon as he left Yvonne and walked to his office, and they would not relent. While he was with patients, he could compartmentalize, but as soon as he was alone in his office, he obsessed over her.

One last time. I should go over and tell her the truth. He rationalized reasons to go see her.

Truth was, he wanted her.

Badly.

He hated wanting her.

Now that he had proposed to Yvonne, the duplicity started to wear on him.

What was he doing?

He tried to busy himself with the afternoon's paperwork. He called Yvonne. Maybe he would stop by her office, instead. No answer. She probably had patients all day.

Shit.

Kadee had texted the previous day a bunch of times. He texted her back to see if she was home, but he didn't even wait for her to respond. He walked over to her place.

Bang. Bang. Bang. He pounded on Kadee's door like a maniac. Standing at her door aroused him. She had better open up and fast.

Kadee opened, let him in, all glow-eyed, happy to see him. "Hey," she said, hugging him, acting casual as though she hadn't texted him twenty-five times yesterday. The woman was clearly obsessed with him.

He grabbed her, kissed her hard, leaned her up against the wall. He ravaged her. Then, like a total dick, as soon as he came, he put his pants on and prepared to leave.

He did have late afternoon patients. He needed to leave.

She screamed and hollered a series of profanities. He felt turned on watching her furious display of passion. Her green eyes flames, her arms flailed all over, the spew of F-words.

He loved Kadee.

The last thing she said: *"Do not come back or I will freaking kill you! OUT! I hate you."*

I hate you, too, Kadee.

When he got outside, he thought, *I think Kadee could kill me. I wouldn't blame her if she did. I probably deserve it.*

When he arrived home after work, Yvonne was in his apartment. She used the key under his mat to let herself in. He jumped when he saw her.

"What's that about? You don't want me here."

"Of course I do. You just surprised me. I wasn't expecting you." He kissed her lips.

"So…" Hands folded in front of her chest, she wiggled her torso. "I found a ring." She exploded with a feverish glee.

Her fervor felt overbearing, like she wanted to swallow him.

A lump sat heavy in his throat. He gulped. "Oh?"

"Yes, handsome." She gushed. "Remember my friend Darcy."

He nodded, yes. He had no idea who Darcy was.

"Well, she reminded me that her cousin was a jeweler and owned a store on Lexington. I went over there between sessions. I know we said we were going together, but I didn't want you to feel pressured with having to deal with your mother. So, I went today. Found the perfect ring. I saw a nice band for you, too, handsome. We can go back this weekend to purchase them." She hugged him. "I've never been so happy."

He hugged her, but the embrace was tentative.

"What is it, handsome? You're disappointed that I went without you?"

"A little. That's OK, though."

She searched his face. "There's something else. What is it?"

"It's nothing."

"Don't 'it's nothing' me." Her lips bunched up like a tulip, her eyes wide with piercing inquisitiveness.

He wanted to be as excited as her. He wanted the promise of his proposal to mean something real, not empty words: a commitment with his heart, not simply some cerebral decision.

He pulled her close, felt the warmth of her body against his. "I'm sorry. It's all happening so fast. I'm overwhelmed with emotion."

"Oh, handsome. You're such a softy. Underneath that cool exterior, you're just a big pussycat. I love that I know that about you."

She released the hug. "So, are we going to dinner with your mother? Was she able to change her plans?"

The dinner was Mother and him alone. Now she included herself.

"No. Surprisingly she wasn't. Which is not a good sign. I know she's up to something."

"Don't worry. Whatever it is, we'll deal with it. Together. Right?"

"Right." He shot her a small smile.

"Take me to dinner."

"Let's stay in. I'm tired from all the excitement and I have a busy day at work tomorrow."

"I'll cook something."

She twirled around, scurried off into the kitchen. The cacophony of pots and pans, the click of the oven being turned on and the refrigerator door opening and closing boomed into the living room. His head pounded.

Meanwhile, Kadee had sent a new string of texts. Hostile, livid texts. *I hate you. Don't ever call me again.* Then followed with conciliatory messages: *Come over. I'm sorry.*

The racket from the kitchen combined with the avalanche of emotion from Kadee made his head spin. He felt suffocated. Part of him wished Yvonne would discover the truth about his duplicity and free him from the prison this secret locked him in. Free him from the grip Kadee still had over him. And maybe even free him from the promise he made to her to spend the rest of his life as an *us*.

He lounged in his recliner staring at the ceiling. It almost looked like it was moving in slow swirls. He tried not to think. But those eerie, taunting voices from his childhood intruded. "Your mama killed your papa. Nah, nah, nah. I heard it's because your mama loved you instead of your papa. Nah, nah, nah." Trucker's hefty voice leading the pack, "Yo, Donovan, I heard you tongue kissed your mother. Is it true, Noah dear? Did you kiss yo mama?"

Streams of tears rolled down Noah's cheeks.

Chapter 23

Late that night while Yvonne slept, Noah lay wide awake. Sick of staring at ceilings every night, he got up and wrote in his journal. He had been writing and writing, almost every night. He ripped most pages out and threw them away. His own words on the pages sometimes felt too real. It felt good to get it out. He would come to the truth, then destroy it. It was a technique Shearstone had recommended. It was a way to get rid of the secrets that tormented him. Noah only used it when he felt particularly plagued by his demons. This thing with Yvonne and Kadee was killing him.

A ticking bomb that could explode at any minute, he felt an ominous tension building. Something awful loomed.

He wrote: *I'm marrying Yvonne. I'm going to make her my wife. Yvonne will be my wife. I have fucked Kadee for the last time. Today was the last time. I really mean it. I hope she doesn't kill me. It's crazy to even think she would kill me. But Mother always told me that women can be evil, that the only woman I can trust is her. Maybe Mother is right. Maybe Kadee is crazy. I'm a man and I'm scared. I'm scared. I will stop fucking her. I must. It's going to be OK. Good night.*

This truth was one he wanted to be real; he wanted to want to marry Yvonne. He loved her. He needed to keep reminding himself because his fears strangled the pleasure out of being with her.

He wrote: *I hate Kadee. She's evil, histrionic and dangerous. I love Kadee. And it terrifies me. She terrifies me. No. I hate Kadee. Fucking hate her. She's twisted my mind into a knot with her passionate nature and sexual provocations. A woman like that cannot be trusted. Despite all of that, I can't stop thinking about her. Sometimes I wish she would come over and say something that would convince me of her love. No. I hate her.*

I love Yvonne. I fear I am not the man she sees.

I hate myself for it.

One lonely tear trickled down his cheek. He tore that page out, ripped it and ripped it until the pieces were too small to rip anymore. He tossed it in the kitchen garbage under the oily remnants of the evening's dinner. He kept the journal underneath an assortment of items in a trunk under his bed. It held mementos from his childhood, mostly things that had belonged to his father.

He listened to Yvonne's breathing, made sure she was sound asleep, stuck the journal under his bed. He would put it back in the trunk when she wasn't in the bedroom. He never wanted her to read it or even know about it, for that matter. That journal and those belongings in the trunk were about the only items he felt were his alone, untainted by

Mother or any other women for that matter. The only truly private place he ever had.

He crawled up next to Yvonne; it felt good to hold her as she slept.

He wanted to be the man she loved.

He would be.

Noah left for work early the next morning. He wished Yvonne would leave with him. But she didn't have patients for a few more hours. So he left her there, in his apartment. It felt uncomfortable leaving her there, but he reminded himself that he planned to marry Yvonne and would no longer have a place of his own. His space would be shared with Yvonne, his soon to be wife.

By the time he arrived at work and had seen two patients, he stopped feeling so discomforted about Yvonne being alone in his place. The idea that she would purposefully violate his privacy was highly unlikely. He trusted her. It would be OK.

Then an hour later, Yvonne called and, suddenly, everything became worse.

"Hi handsome. You have a quick minute?"

"A quick one, yes."

"Your mother called me and insisted we have dinner tomorrow night. She and I. Without you. She said she thinks we should get to know each other on a more personal level since I am going to be her daughter-in-law."

Noah plopped into his office chair. A burst of heat coursed through him. "I'll come with you."

"No. No. I think this is a good thing. I really do. Maybe she's already coming around."

"She's not. Trust me on this. She's up to something."

"Perhaps you're right, handsome. But we have to deal with her sooner or later. And she's barking up the wrong tree if she thinks she's going to bully and threaten me out of marrying you. The love of my life."

He took a heavy breath. "I suppose you're right. She's not going to let up until you meet her. Let me know where you're eating. I'll meet you after dinner."

"That sounds like a good compromise. So, I'll come over tonight after work."

"I have a meeting with J.C. I won't be done until around 9. I'll text you when I'm on my way home, and you can meet me there."

"I'll go to yoga class, then, and come over afterward. No need to text. I'll be waiting for you when you get home. Love you."

Noah unbuttoned the top of his shirt. "Love you, too."

"Toodles."

He immediately called Mother and asked her about the dinner. She acted all innocent, gave him the same story she had given to Yvonne: She wanted to spend time alone with Yvonne, get to know her soon-to-be daughter-in-law.

He did not trust her.

"Mother, you know it's over between me and Kadee and has been for a while. Please do not mention Kadee to Yvonne." Then he manipulated Mother using one of her own ploys. "Let it be *our* little secret. Something that only you and I share."

Practically verbatim what Mother had said when she told him about father and the berries.

"OK, dear. Our secret. My lips are sealed."

Then like a reflex, no thought, no conscious decision, he texted Kadee: *Are you around tonight around 7:00? I'll come over so we can talk.*

An hour later when he checked his phone between appointments, she had responded: *Yes. See you then.*

His mind felt like a circus of emotion when he ambled his way over to Kadee's that evening. He feared his own lack of control. He didn't want to go. Yet, he felt helpless against this pull she had over him. By the time he arrived at her apartment he was enraged at her for having this grip on him. He ripped her clothes off with a hungry, violent forcefulness. The overwhelming passion, which felt desperate and furious to him, made every thrust into her more and more aggressive.

She seemed to like it, too; it made the fury even stronger; he pushed further and further into her.

Then, as soon as he finished, he put his clothes on to leave. Her powerful screams scared him — and turned him on. "If you come back, I swear to God I will kill you, you pathetic loser. I hate you."

He grabbed her face, squeezed it, planted a hard kiss on her lips. "I love you, you whore."

She squirmed out of his grip, slapped his hand. "OUT!" She hollered and the word reverberated off her walls.

"I won't be coming back. I never want to see you again." He stuck his face right up to hers. "Ever."

"Good," she said, and tears gushed down her cheeks. "You are a bad man."

You're right, Kadee with a D.
I am.

When he got home, Yvonne was there. His blue pajama shirt buttoned up to her neck. She sat on his recliner writing in a notebook, looking pure and angelic. "Hi, handsome." She gushed. Those baby blues lit up and beaming.

I am a bad man.

"Hi beautiful." He kissed her. "I want to take a quick shower."

He had to get the smell of his ugly indiscretion off of him.

When he got out of the shower, Yvonne lay in bed, the sheet turned down on his side. She patted the empty space. "Come, handsome. I'm making my wedding guest list. It's preliminary. I just want to have an idea of how many people so we know the size of the loft we need. Here." She handed him the notebook. "Can you write down your list?"

"Can I do it tomorrow, beautiful? I'm wiped out from the day and I feel a headache coming on." He kissed her cheek.

Her nostrils expanded and contracted once, twice, thrice. "OK. I understand. You've had a long day."

Noah clicked the television on.

Yvonne's nostrils flared again. And again. And again. Noah flipped through the channels, settling on the news.

"This OK with you?"

"Yes." She said in a feeble voice.

He knew she was pissed, but he could not deal with her needs right then. He needed to deal with his own, which included not thinking about anything that was happening around him or how much he despised himself.

They watched the news in silence, each on their own side of the bed. When it ended, he handed Yvonne the remote. "Put on whatever you want."

She landed on the movie *Unfaithful*. "Oh, I so enjoy Richard Gere. I do feel bad for him in this movie. I really do." She snuggled up against Noah, stuck her head right into the nook of his underarm, leaned against his torso. "This is nice."

He kissed the top of her head, "It is."

He tried his best to ignore the irony and watch the movie with Yvonne, his fiancée.

Chapter 24

You are a bad man, Noah Donovan.

The following day after work, Noah walked over to Kadee's.

Yvonne had her dinner with mother. This would be the last time he would see Kadee. She had texted that morning. *I'm sorry I yelled at you. Call me so we can talk.*

Like her little puppet, he called her back. Then, he made her a promise, he knew he would break: *Yes, I will stay over tonight.*

If she insisted upon reeling him in, gripping him with her sexual provocations, then he would treat her like the whore that she was. He'd go over, fuck her one last time, leave with enough time to spare to make it to the restaurant to meet Yvonne and Mother.

An unforeseen obstacle presented itself when he arrived at Kadee's: Her best friend, Vanessa, was there. On Kadee's couch, arms folded, one leg crossed over the other, her planted foot tapped the floor. Vanessa, with her curly hair and olive skin, shot him a fierce, knowing look. She knew who he was. And he saw his self-distain through her eyes as she glared at him.

Unlike Kadee or Yvonne, both still under the spell of love's adulation, Vanessa knew what Noah was. Underneath his suave, meticulously crafted persona, Vanessa knew as well as he did that he was nothing. He was a person who hadn't a clue who he was or what he wanted, a person who manipulated anyone who had the misfortune of becoming attached to him. In one piercing glower, he saw the truth in Vanessa's eyes.

Nevertheless, he shot her his best magnanimous smile. "You must be Vanessa." Certainly, he would get points for recognizing her even though they had never formally met.

Those arms remained folded across her chest, the foot tap became faster and harder. Then he reached his hand out, left it in front of her face until, with a heavy breath, she reached out and shook it.

Another fierce glare and she said, "Yes, I am. I'd like to say it's a good guess, but – "

"Well it's a pleasure to finally meet you."

He had to get rid of her and that smug expression of triumph. That look reminded him that no matter what he did or said, as long as she remained in his presence, she would be a proverbial mirror showing him what an actual piece of crap he really was.

He bantered politely with her for another minute. Vanessa, Kadee's watchdog, gave him shit because she had never met him. "Kadee's boyfriend," she called him using air quotes. *Blah, blah, blah,* was all he heard after that, because he remained preoccupied with his primary mission: Coax Kadee into the bedroom and charm her into throwing Vanessa, and that self-satisfied, victorious look of hers, out of her apartment so they could be alone.

A natural at manipulating Kadee, he got her to toss her friend out without much effort. All he had to do was give that false promise, again: *I promise to stay tonight. Just ask her to leave so we can be alone.*

A promise and a guarantee weren't the same thing. Promises were merely a spoken contract between two people, one of whom trusted the other at their word. Promises were meant to be broken.

Kadee went back into the living room. He remained in the bedroom waiting for her to come back in. Vanessa, *what a sweetheart,* she hollered a series of creative profanities, purposefully loud, so she knew he would hear. "He's a worthless piece of shit. And a psychopath. A shitty, pathetic, psychopath. And I'm going to make sure he pays for what he's doing to you."

Clearly, Vanessa had the same artful affinity for overblown displays of emotion as Kadee had. "Psychopath" was a bit harsh, the "worthless piece of shit" and "shitty" and "pathetic," however, were unfortunately accurate. He respected Vanessa's precision.

Vanessa left with a door slam.

He quickly stripped. Lying naked, he held a vibrator he wanted Kadee to use while he watched her. Kadee came in, looked at him, then the vibrator. "Come on DeeDee. I want to watch you."

She seemed reticent for a second, but quickly gave in. She used the vibrator and he felt turned on as she massaged herself. Those *bunk-bunk* hips straddled the vibrator, and he felt his thickness expand. He wanted to ravage her furiously. He took her from behind this time. He felt the force of his virility. While inside Kadee, he was a God, every inadequacy he ever felt — gone, washed away, forgotten. He shoved in harder. She nudged him, suggested through soft rubs that he needed to be gentler.

But he pushed even harder, in and out, reckless, vicious, free. Pushing in as hard as he wanted to push her away.

A long blast released from him; they both panted from the ferocity of the experience. "That was great!" he exclaimed.

"Um huh." She took his arms and wrapped them around her. The squabbling over his soon to be broken promise loomed as soon as he told her he was leaving.

Kadee's neediness had become as predictable and overbearing as mother. He relished in the ability to know what to expect. If nothing else, he could predict the violence of the female gender. He was a human compass when it came to gauging the hysterical, controlling, suffocating female. That wasn't a small thing.

She screamed and hollered as he got dressed to leave. A shoe — thankfully not a stiletto heel — flew across the room and hit him on the shoulder. No big deal. He was a grown man. It would take more than a furious shoe to knock him down.

He then made another false promise, "I'll come back in a couple hours."

"Fine. Whatever. You're the one in charge, right?" Her eyes looked nearly frozen with a desperate fury, like he had never seen on her before.

He kissed her cheek, turned and left.

I hate you, Kadee. You get what you deserve.

Kadee didn't even scream this time when he walked out. The hallway silence was deafening as he exited — the quiet before the storm.

He stepped outside. Checked his phone. Yvonne had texted: *I don't know where you are, but you need to come now! Something has happened.*

Something has happened.
That can't be good.

Chapter 25

Worse than expected. He arrived at the restaurant, Yvonne and Mother stared at each other in a standoff. The air was thick and riddled with conflict. He sat down, kissed Mother then Yvonne, watching them observe his every move. He ran a hand through his hair, which had a few knots from his frolic with Kadee.

"What is it?" He was sweating. "Mother?" He asked, his voice thin.

He almost didn't want to know. The heaviness that hung at that table felt tangible; the pressure hurt. Mother and Yvonne sat with severe eyes glued to each other. Mother didn't break the gaze, but rubbed his thigh. Finally, in a saccharine tone, said, "Yvonne and I were discussing some things." Mother overenunciated "things," purposefully using a general and generic word, rather than telling him what they discussed. It was a way to toy with him.

She rubbed his leg again.

Then, the stunning disclosure of "things" came when Yvonne threw an envelope in front of him. Her nostrils were huge, pulsating in and out and in and out.

Yvonne was fuming, so whatever was in the envelope could not be good.

He opened the envelope. A series of photographs. His heart accelerated as he looked through them. Pictures of Kadee and him, a visual diary of their relationship: Kadee and him hailing a taxi, Kadee and him at an outside café, Kadee and him in Bryant Park, drinking coffee, laughing, holding hands, three of the pictures showed them kissing.

Hooooly crap!

"Your mother brought these for me." Yvonne's voice was contained, but he heard the pierce. "She wanted me to see… she wanted me to know," she took a heavy breath. "She wanted to make sure I knew about this woman, about you and Kadee."

He broke out in a sweat. His eyes narrow, his brow a V.

Think, Donovan, you shitty, pathetic loser.

"But I told her that I already knew about her, that you had told me ages ago."

He looked at Yvonne, ran his fingers through his hair. In a hesitant voice, he said to Yvonne, "Right… of course."

He did not deserve Yvonne. His mind spun with all the different scenarios of what actually went down. But one thing seemed clear, Yvonne protected him, them, from Mother.

And he didn't deserve her.

"Mother, where did these come from? Where did you get these?"

"Well, I took them, dear. Mother took them." Of course, Mother said it without an ounce of consideration for the fact that she completely and utterly invaded his privacy. Noooo… Mother decided she had the right to take photos of him without his knowledge.

"You took them? I'm confused, Mother. You followed me?"

Then Mother, unabashedly and with a huff, said that following Noah was beneath her standards. Rather, Mother, a self-proclaimed epitome of dignity and class, hired someone to follow him and take the pictures. Then she generously admonished him, using a tone so overly sweet it sounded bitter. "If you marry Yvonne there will be no more money. Dear."

Furious, he took Yvonne's hand and rose from the table.

Mother pulled his forearm with the grip of a strong man, practically spitting at him when she spoke. "Did you hear what I said? If you marry Yvonne, there will be no more money."

"I heard you, Mother." He kissed her cheek. He hated her. "We can talk about this later."

"No, we won't, dear. If you leave now, there will be nothing to talk about. If you leave now, there will be no more money."

He was so sick of her grip on him. "I'm a successful doctor, Mother. I don't need your money. I'll talk to you later."

He took Yvonne's hand, left Mother abandoned at the table. Her eyes held the look of a rabid dog as she watched her son leave with another woman.

No words were had between Yvonne and Noah the entire walk back to his place. Their cadence synchronized into a perfectly matched stern determination, each for their own reasons. Flabbergasted by Mother's audacity — why, he wasn't sure; Mother was capable of just about anything; she had killed his father for crying out loud. But to have him followed and using the information to destroy his future seemed outrageous, even for her.

Underestimating Mother was a big mistake.

This was not his biggest problem, though. His biggest problem: How to explain the surreptitious relationship with Kadee. He didn't know how much of the truth Yvonne knew, so it was hard to know what he should disclose in an attempt to wheedle his way out of the hole he was now in, and to convince the woman he wanted to spend his life with that she could trust him.

If she left him, he deserved it.

Tears trickled out of Yvonne's eyes as soon as they were inside his apartment. Her voice quivered. "How could you? How could you violate the promise of our bond with a careless indiscretion? Noah. I trusted you with my heart, and you have shattered it into itsy- bitsy pieces."

Watching her, he felt nothing. Nothing. He loved her, how could he feel nothing.

Maybe he was a psychopath.

Tongue-tied, he fumbled for words, "I– I–." Something, he had to say something. Suddenly, he felt frightened, frightened that he would lose Yvonne. "It– It started while we were just friends. I'm so sorry. I have been trying to end it. But this woman, Kadee, she's unstable and threatened to kill herself." He made his eyes soft and pained. "I didn't love her. Or even want anything to do with her, but I was concerned she would kill herself. So, I tried to back out slowly. I wanted to tell you, but I was scared. I love you so much. The thought of losing you was too much."

She watched him talk, hung on his every word. She sucked her cheeks in, released. Sucked them in, released. Stared at him with an anguished look. "I don't believe you," she said in a hollow voice.

"What can I say? Please. I'm telling you the truth."

"I want to believe you, Noah. I really do. Unfortunately, I am not sure that I can. I know things that I wish I didn't."

"What things."

"Things that I can't tell you."

"Secrets?"

"Not secrets as much as inside information. A type of secret." She narrowed her eyes, gave him a steely look. "Let's just say, I know things about Kadee."

"What things? What are you talking about? Do you know Kadee."

"I can't say." Another steely look.

"Were you following me, too?"

"No. Noah. Don't you know me at all? I would never violate your privacy like that. You have always taken me and my love for granted. You don't know how to be loved. Not in any real way."

"You're right. But I want to try harder. Please, Yvonne. Please. We can work this out. You are the only woman — person — I have ever trusted. Besides my father. Please."

"I need time to think. I will call you tomorrow."

"Are you leaving me?"

"No. I don't know. Maybe. I love you, however unfortunate that may be. And I want to believe that you were planning to leave this woman. I need to believe that. I need time to think. You must give me that."

"I will. I love you, Yvonne. I want to be the man you see when you look at me. I want to be the man who you love."

"I know. I really do."

Chapter 26

Yvonne was angry. Mother was angry. Kadee was angry.

Noah insisted on making things right! So, he initiated a barrage of email exchanges with mother as soon as Yvonne left. For whatever twisted reason — one he didn't understand — he wanted Mother to forgive him for asserting his independence.

His world was crumbling around him. It felt the way it had the day his father died, like nothing made sense anymore. He panicked. Nothing would ever be right again.

His first email to Mother begged for her forgiveness.

Mother, I've been naughty, I know. I shouldn't have left you in the restaurant. I'm sorry. Will you please forgive me?

He hated himself.

She waited more than an hour before responding: *You have not listened to Mother. Haven't I taught you anything? Women are evil. They can't be trusted. They will only hurt you. You must believe Mother. I wouldn't do anything to hurt you. You are my baby boy. All*

I ever wanted to do was protect you. But if you don't leave her, you will be sorry. Love, Mother.

He stewed reading her response. *Protect me? Never hurt me? Hurt me is all Mother has ever done.* His rage boiled over. And he felt frantic to gain her forgiveness. His stomach was in knots.

He wrote her back. He hated begging, but he had to plead for her forgiveness. He needed it. Mother would never show any mercy, though. He knew it even as he tried to receive it.

Mother was Mother.

She wrote back, insisting he end it with Yvonne or he would be sorry.

He tried calling her.

No answer.

Just the voicemail. He didn't bother leaving a message. Everything he had to say was in the emails.

God forbid mother ever did anything in the interest of anyone else's wants or needs. He had spent his whole life under her reign. Because of that, he didn't even know how to love someone who actually loved him. He had learned a twisted, tormented kind of love filled with pain and exploitation. But Yvonne's devotion had been like a boulder in a wild, formidable river, standing strong against the powerful rushing water. She stood firm, unwavering. The promise of being there had been proven through the years. She stayed no matter what — a Zen space in his life, the quiet strength behind every good thing he did from the first day he met her. Yet, he managed to dislodge this enduring person who was as committed to her place in his life as the boulder in the churning river. With one careless action, he forced her out of her space, causing her to careen away from him.

You are a bad man, he heard Kadee's voice say.

You get what you deserve, Donovan.

No! He could not lose Yvonne.

He paced around his apartment and thought of calling Yvonne. He decided to write in his journal, instead. He wanted to be clear in his thoughts. Everything coalesced: Mother, his father's death, his feelings for Kadee, his feelings for Yvonne, his true feelings about himself. Who was he? What did he want? What was he doing? Worry and doubt about his future crowded his thoughts.

So, he wrote.

I hate my life. I hate myself. The secrets from my past haunt my present. I feel dirty. I feel ashamed. No one can ever see who I really am. I don't even know who I really am.

I love Yvonne. She's the only woman I've ever loved, purely and without complications. But the way she sees me is not accurate. The look in her eyes when she gazes at me terrifies me. She sees a man that I am not. That I can never be. If she finds out the truth, she'll be as disgusted as I am. I can't let her see behind my façade I hide behind. I can't let her see the small, nothingness that I really am. I want to be the man she sees. Oh, how I want to be that man. If she gives me another chance, I will be that man. I had read once that love heals. If I let myself feel her love, I will be healed. I will become who she sees. I promise. I will.

I admit that I loved Kadee. I hate admitting it, but it's the truth. If I'm going to come clean, I must admit it here, in my journal, if nowhere else. Subversive, overly emotional and too sexy to ever trust, I loved that woman more than I ever knew I was capable of loving. I hated loving her. She represented a side of life that I always imagined: to be free, to be cheeky, to be proud and uninhibited. Kadee is everything I aspire to be, and am not, nor will I ever be. But she enchanted me. I blamed her for making me love her, and it's HER fault. She made me love her, but not in a cunning, manipulative way, not in a Mother-way. She was just being herself, so I fell for her. And I wound up hating her for it. I hated her for making me love her to the point that I was terrified she would destroy me and my life. And in a way, hasn't she? I hated her for being able to be so carefree in the way she lives, casual and natural, rebellious. You can never trust someone who doesn't give much care or thought to what others think. Kadee was unsafe. And still is. I will never see her again — I hope. I will probably love her for the rest of my life and hate her for it. Kadee, you slutty bitch, you got what you wanted — I may never recover from you. Forever a victim of abandoning myself to an unsafe woman. I got what I deserved, Kadee with a D.

Now that I've cleared up the Kadee debacle, I can go to Yvonne and plead with her for another chance. I want to marry Yvonne. She will love me wholly and unconditionally. I still don't know how to love that way. But through her, I will learn. Please, Yvonne, forgive me. Forgive me. If you don't, I will never forgive myself, and I already carry the burden of blame for my father's death. Please don't make me carry another emotional burden. I'm not sure I can.

Tears streamed down Noah's cheeks as he wrote: grief from his lost childhood, his lost innocence, the loss of his father, the loss of ever having a loving mother, and now, the awareness of his inability to love himself or anyone else in a healthy way.

He tore that page out, ripped it with a violent intensity, tearing the pages to bits as a way to destroy the despised part of himself. Tears continued to roll down his cheeks. He tried to fight them off.

If Yvonne forgave him, he would get his new beginning. A chance to heal the wounds he had carried his whole life. He would be open, he would trust her, love her unconditionally, be worthy of her trust.

In the heat of desperation at 3 a.m., he called Yvonne.

She answered groggy, "Hello"

"Please. Please. Let me come over. I'm dying inside. Please." He gushed.

"OK. OK. Come. But it doesn't mean I'm ready to forgive you, yet."

"Thank you. I understand, beautiful."

His eyes zigzagged around the apartment as he tried to find his jeans in a hurry. He found them, threw them on, ran out without stopping to think through anything. On autopilot and on his way to win back the woman he loved.

On his way to Yvonne's, he promised himself he would never see Kadee again. He deleted her number from his phone. If she called or texted him, he would immediately erase the messages and her number.

He loved Kadee so much that he hated her. That was not a good thing, so he knew he could never see her again.

Yvonne answered the door, half-asleep. "Come in," she said in a hoarse voice. She barely looked at him. He tried to talk, but she said, "Not now." He didn't push it. She let him in the apartment; the door of possibility was open, at least.

She did let him sleep next to her, even allowed him to hold her, but her body remained taut and closed off. She would not kiss him back when he kissed her, either.

Years and years to get her to open up to him; in one minute, they were back to where they had started when he screwed her over in medical school.

You are a complete idiot, Donovan. How did you think this was going to end?

The next morning, Noah had early patients. Yvonne curled up in bed, covers up to her neck. Her eyes followed him as he fumbled to put his jeans and shoes on. He didn't want to leave her. His eyes filled with emotion when he sat on the bed, brushing the wisps of brown hairs away from her face. "I'm sorry," he said and his voice cracked.

She looked at him, said nothing.

"Do you have patients today?"

"Yes."

"Can I come back tonight? To talk. Please, Yvonne."

"I'll be home by seven. You can come back. But, Noah, I don't know if I can forgive you. I'm willing to try, but sometimes when we want to get past something, no matter how hard we try, we can't. Sometimes the hurt is too great and the emotional damage can't be undone. I loved you with my whole heart and trusted you with my feelings. But you broke me." She sat up in bed, her words more fervent. "In an instant, you shattered the trust that took us thirteen years to build. Now you're asking me to trust you again. For a third time. And I'm not sure yet if I'm willing to try. I need time."

He took a sharp breath, held her hand. "I understand."

She averted his eyes, but not before he recognized the pain in them, a tormented and languished gaze, a stare preserved for people who were able to love deeply enough that they could be destroyed by it. For a moment, he knew that gaze intimately, remembering it from a time long gone. The ache of a shattered belief once known. He knew that feeling. It was the way he felt the night Mother and his father argued about him. The night his father found out about Mother and his clandestine relationship.

That first night mother crawled into bed with him when he was only six years old, she had said, "You must never tell your father about our special nights together or that Mother loves you more than him. Understand, dear?" He felt her breasts soft against his back. He nodded yes, but he felt uncomfortable. Feeling her breasts against him felt good, but if it needed to be a secret, he knew it was bad.

His father had told him to always tell the truth, never lie. His secret with Mother felt like a lie because he had to keep the truth from his father. He remembered the night his parents fought over him, his father's words that Mother sleeping with him naked was inappropriate, that his father had to take Noah away to keep him safe from Mother. His world collapsed around him. This secret relationship Mother and he shared — his most intimate — was all he knew of love and closeness.

What he trusted to be authentic love was a lie. He loved and trusted Mother, completely, and she took advantage of that. She did bad things to him and made him enjoy it. It was that day when he realized he could never trust people or himself. Love was just an act people portrayed to get things they needed. He acted like he loved Mother because he was dependent on her. By the time he was a teenager, he realized Mother acted like she loved him to get things from him.

He knew nothing of love that involved trust, pure unguarded abandon. That capacity was lost the day he realized love made people vulnerable and being vulnerable could break a person in half.

Yvonne loved him completely, and it ruined her. *He* ruined her.

Looking at that pain in her eyes, he felt a closeness with her that he had never experienced before. Like they shared something powerful and unspoken, something so deep and devastating, it bonded them together. He knew then, that if Yvonne didn't forgive him, he would never survive.

He was nothing without her.

"I love you, Yvonne." He kissed her forehead. He wished he could give her back what he had taken – her ability to trust that her love would not be exploited. The wince, the ache, the agony: He saw them all coalesce on her face; he wished he could take it away. He would do whatever he had to in order to repair what had been broken. No more secrets.

She said nothing as he walked out. He turned, said, "I'll see you tonight."

She nodded.

The day at work was terrible. Lethargy overcame him and it took every effort to focus on his patients. He didn't have the type of job which allowed for emotional distraction. He needed to be focused. Yvonne had called a few times during the day, left messages. A couple said, *"I don't know if I can forgive you."* A little while later, *"I love you. I do want to forgive you."*

Kadee texted a bunch of times: *Please come over,* then *I hate you, you freaking bastard.*

Clearly he had an aptitude for making women drive him crazy with mixed messages.

Mother still refused to see him if he didn't leave Yvonne. He refused to indulge Mother's wishes, remaining steadfast that he planned to marry Yvonne — if she would still have him. At least Mother was consistent. He could always count on Mother for that.

Maybe she would call him later. Maybe.

You get what you deserve, Donovan.

Chapter 27

That night at Yvonne's: a complete catastrophe. Yvonne's secret was worse than he could have ever imagined.

Yvonne went out to pick up wine, leaving Noah in her apartment. Yvonne, who was always so meticulous with details, was emotionally distraught and had forgotten her cell phone.

Her phone vibrated and vibrated, a string of text messages came through. He didn't mean to look, but it sat on the coffee table right next to him. When he happened to glance at it, his eyes grew wide. His heart began beating so wildly, he could feel the blood pumping in his neck. He grabbed the phone, his hands shaking. He found a string of texts from Kadee's phone number.

Yvonne's phone had a lock on it, but he could read the new texts as they popped up.

Dr. Tracy, things are really bad. Can I come in earlier this week for my session?

He has been coming over. I keep texting him.
I'm so upset. I need to see you.
Please let me know if you have any earlier availability this week.
Thank you.
Hooooly Shit!

Noah sat nearly paralyzed, unable to process the information. *Kadee is texting Yvonne for help? Yvonne is her therapist? What? How long has Yvonne known about my relationship with Kadee? Has Yvonne been keeping secrets from me?*

Noooo... it couldn't be. Must be a mistake.

He sat upright on the couch, waiting for Yvonne to return.

Yvonne walked in, immediately noticing his posture. "What is it?"

She saw her cell phone on the coffee table. She looked at the phone, then Noah, then back. She turned pale, grabbed the phone, scanned the texts.

Noah sat taut. "Did you know before Mother told you?"

"Nope."

"How could you not know? Kadee is your patient. *You've* been keeping secrets from *me!* Lying!" His eyes widened. "You and she have been plotting against me. Playing with my head!"

"Noah. That is absolutely nuts." Her nostrils flared, anger seething to the surface, but her voice remained collected. "You have been sleeping with Kadee, for God knows how long, and you're blaming this on me? On us?"

"How could you not have known? Just tell me that!"

"I shouldn't even be telling you this. Nor do I feel you have even earned the right for an explanation. But for some reason, she used a different name. She has been calling you Aaron in our therapy sessions, so I had no idea. But you see, now *I* can put all of the itsy-bitsy pieces together. Stories she told me about Aaron were really stories about you. I know things I wish I didn't. A lot of things." She sucked in her cheeks, then released them with a *pop*. "Unless, of course, you and she were conspiring against me."

"No. Noooo. Never. I would never do that to you."

"Unfortunately, it's hard to believe anything you say. I want to believe you. I really do."

He went to pull her close, but with a flat expression and a stoic voice she said, "I think you should leave now."

"Please, Yvonne. I've made a terrible mistake. Please. Kadee was suicidal. I'm sure you knew that since you see her professionally. I couldn't risk having her death on my hands. That's why I still saw her and talked to her. I never loved her. I proposed to you. Please."

"I can't talk about this right now. I want to forgive you. I really do. But I need more time."

"More time. Does that mean you will forgive me?"

"I hope so. But I don't know. I really don't. I need time alone right now. I'd like you to leave. We can talk later or tomorrow. I'm going into my room. When I come out, I expect you to be gone. Please respect my wishes." She turned, hummed softly. She went into her bedroom, closed the door behind her.

A minute later Evanescence's, "My Immortal" blasted from her room. Glasses on a shelf next to her room shook. Yvonne sang loudly in a shrill tone. It pierced his ears.

She sang along with Amy Lee. Lines about pain that was too deep to heal.

He wanted to die. If it was really over, he would die. He was worthless. Without Yvonne, he was nothing. A torrent of chaos poured through his veins, a tornado of emotion. His fisted hand suspended in front of Yvonne's bedroom door, he wanted to knock, beg her to let him in, to forgive him.

She made the music louder, sang louder. Lines about deep emotional pain that no amount of time could heal. It cut him to the core. He looked at his fist hovering at her door, slumped his shoulders in defeat. She wasn't ready to forgive him. If nothing else, he had to respect her need for space.

You get what you deserve, Donovan.
And you don't get what you don't deserve. You don't deserve her.
Maybe you get exactly what you expect.

He ambled toward his apartment, shoulders slumped, feeling crushed, beaten.

He wanted to call Kadee. He wanted to ask her about this relationship she had with Yvonne. Maybe she knew about Yvonne and went to see her as a purposeful ploy. Kadee, that bitch, found out about Yvonne and pretended to be Yvonne's patient, so she could disclose their relationship to

Yvonne under the rouse of a private therapy session. Yvonne would have to sit there, a neutral party, listening to Kadee talk about *him*. Livid, he turned around and stormed toward Kadee's apartment. This clearly was her fault. He wanted to hear Kadee tell him the truth. With hungry, furious steps he marched toward her place.

The night was breezy. As he turned down her street, a gentle gust blew back at him. A few leaves circled near the ground, faint dust flurried about. Tears licked the edges of his eyes. Anger. Confusion. Desperation. He was almost to her apartment, ready to yell at her, when he felt his phone vibrate against his side. His hands fumbled as he went into the pocket of his sweatshirt.

Yvonne. A text: *Let's talk tomorrow evening. I'd really like to try to figure this out. I just need a little time.*

His palms, thick with sweat, puckered against the phone as he wrote back. *OK, beautiful. Whatever you need. See you tomorrow.*

On the corner of Kadee's street, he couldn't decide if he should go to her place or not. He walked a few steps down her block, did an about-face, walked the same few steps away from her apartment. He did that a few times, pacing her block like a sentry guarding his emotions.

A pack of giggling, boisterous twenty-something girls passed by. One with a tight dress and huge platforms shot him a flirty glance. "You need directions, mistah? You look lost." Her friends burst out laughing; a wave of alcohol filled his nostrils.

"I'm good." He deserved every ounce of ridicule he received, but not from a bunch of slutty, drunk girls.

Those girls did snap him out of his indecision, though. He could never talk to Kadee again, he realized with clarity. If things were ever going to be right with Yvonne, he had to trust Yvonne's word. She had said Kadee came to her for therapy and used a fake name. It seemed odd. Maybe Kadee knew he knew Yvonne; they had gone to the same medical school. Yvonne had her diplomas up on her office wall. Maybe Kadee lied to Yvonne about his name because she thought they were possibly friends or something like that.

If Kadee knew he had an intimate relationship with Yvonne — if Kadee knew the truth — he was positive she would have said something to him. Kadee was impetuous, not one to hold back emotions. If anything, she could use a few classes in emotional self-control. Still, it was odd.

Oddness didn't matter, because now that he knew Kadee and Yvonne had a relationship, he realized that any interactions he had with Kadee would go back to Yvonne. Dragging his feet, emotionally exhausted and physically weary, he stumbled home. Yvonne and he would talk tomorrow. At least he had that hope.

Once in his apartment, he couldn't stop ruminating over the latest discovery: They knew each other! And who knew what Kadee told Yvonne. He wanted to vomit. His stomach grumbled, but he fought it off until the feeling dissipated. He guzzled a glass of water before sliding into bed. The ceiling seemed to circle round and round as he stared at it, trying his best not to think about what Kadee told Yvonne in their therapy sessions.

The *briiing* of his phone ringing jolted him. *Mother,* he thought sickened by the thought of her. A burst of pure fury coursed through him and, suddenly, he was glad that she called. This offered him the opportunity to scream at her.

Blood rushed to his face. He picked up, hollered, "Mother. I'm glad you've called. I am so sick– "

"Noah, dear. Do not yell at Mother."

"I– I– " He got out of bed and paced the room.

"Noah. I love you more than anyone else will ever love you. You are turning your back on Mother. This is a big mistake." And then, "Remember the secret I told you about the berries?"

He took a sharp breath. His steps halted. "Yes."

"Well, dear, the truth is that it was Mother's idea to give your father the berries. He had no idea. Alas. Poor dear. I couldn't have him take you away from me. So I did what any mother in my position would do. I took care of it."

"Mother!" He yelled. Tears of pain and rage welled in his eyes.

"I will do what I have to do now."

"What are you saying, Mother?"

"Nothing dear. Nothing at all. Except that you should never underestimate Mother's love."

What did she mean? Would she hurt Yvonne? Kadee? Even him? He would kill her before he let that happen.

"Mother, I'll consider what you're saying. Can we meet for dinner and discuss it in a day or two."

"If you end it with her first, dear."

"Yes, Mother. I know."

"Good, dear. Call Mother when it's done. Oh, and just so you know, Mother placed a container under your desk, too. There are video recordings of you having sex with Kadee, Yvonne and some other whores. You really are a reckless and careless boy. Mother has tried her very best to educate you on the hazards of becoming involved with the wrong woman. Clearly, you have not listened."

"What? Mother, how could— "

"Mother knows everything you've been up to. She thought your two girlfriends might want to know too. And, I put some pictures of Mother in there also."

"What? You X-ed out your own picture? Why would you do that?"

"Ah, you found the container. Good. Mother did that to show you that no matter how much you try to hide things from her, she will always find out the truth. You tried to cross Mother out of your life with your foolish secrets. You haven't learned, dear. You can't keep secrets from Mother."

"Mother, this is beyond— "

Click.

She was unbelievable. Maybe even insane. Mother took videos of him. What was she talking about? She had to be toying with him, trying to get him to do what she wanted: end the relationship with Yvonne. She was responsible for the container that Kadee found, though. And Kadee was furious at whatever she saw on those memory sticks. Would Mother be sick enough to record him? And how would she do it? Did she have a camera hooked up in his room? Did she know everything he was doing behind his closed bedroom door? He was so furious, he could kill her. But first, he would get to the bottom of her exploits by manipulating her into seeing him and confronting her face-to-face.

Worse than that, and that was already unspeakable, Mother had plotted and killed his father because of him. Now Mother threatened to hurt Yvonne? Or him? The woman was capable of anything. He remembered that looked of shattered truth that he shared with Yvonne.

Mother had done it to him, again. To betray a trust he had for her that he didn't even know he had. Even after everything she had done over the years, a part of him still trusted her enough that she could violate and exploit him. A bottomless rage welled up inside him, a violent wave of heat so intense he thought he might explode.

The floor felt uneven as he stumbled into the living room. His thoughts were tangled and tormented. Mother had to be stopped. He would kill her if he had to. He cracked open a fresh bottle of tequila, drank a shot, then another, then another. He had to stop the endless pain that permeated him. He hated mother. He hated himself. The two thoughts were so woven together, he couldn't separate his self-hate from his hate for her.

Blurry from the alcohol, slurred words and flaccid limbs, he staggered to his recliner. Almost tripped over his own feet a few times. He passed out in a restless, drunken sleep.

The next day, after work, he went home to lay down. Exhaustion from the stress, the alcohol, and the poor sleep overwhelmed him. Kadee had spent the morning sending him a series of texts, some livid, some conciliatory. One said: *I hate you so much, I could kill you.* A few minutes after that, *I'm sorry. Come over. Please.* He wanted to call her, badly. He wanted to know the goddamn truth. Did she know about Yvonne?

Worse, he wanted to see her. He wasn't sure how much longer he could resist the temptation. If she would stop with the endless texts, maybe he could get the woman out of his mind.

Yvonne had called him in the late morning, left a voicemail while he was with patients, said she would call again around six o'clock. He wanted to feel more rested when they talked. Nothing had ever felt this important.

Although what he thought he wanted to say changed that morning. A new thought had begun to formulate in his mind, and it was something he felt more strongly about as the day went on. A way to make things right.

If he really loved Yvonne, he would let her go. Let her find someone who could love her the way she deserved. He wanted to be that man, but he was nothing inside, an empty shell. Maybe the best way to make things right was to turn his back on her, pretend he didn't want her anymore. So, she would be free of him and his tortured, tainted love.

His love was poison.

The more he let the idea sink in, the more certain he felt that that's what he needed to do. An action of true love, a selfless act he would do with only her interest at heart. With that he drifted into a light sleep. A clanging in the bathroom startled him a couple of hours later, waking him. It almost sounded like the toilet overflowed.

Half dazed, he went in. With maniacal, anguished eyes, she glared at him. Her hand, a maze of purple veins, gripped a huge butcher knife. Before he could react, the knife was pressed against his chest. The edge of the blade glimmered under the bathroom light.

Blindsided, he stumbled back. "I — No." He backed up. He could feel the sharp, cold blade threatening to breach his warm skin.

"Yes," she said through clutched teeth.

"I'm sorry. Please! Don't kill me." He said, but even as he stared at her, terrified, frozen, he knew he deserved it.

She licked her lips. Her eyes morphed from crazed to vacant, as though her self-awareness had left her. The tip of the blade pressed in his bare chest. A drop of blood popped out, silhouetted against the gleaming metal. He tried to wrestle the knife away from her, but she was strong. She pushed the tip in hard, plunging the rest of the blade into his chest. It hurt like nothing he ever felt before. She yanked out the knife. Blood flowed from his chest like a red river.

He grabbed at his chest, collapsed onto his knees, then fell to the ground. She stabbed him in the back of his shoulder blade. A scream built up at the back of his throat, but he didn't have the strength to get it out. He struggled to roll over. Her wanted to see her face again. Once on his back, pain everywhere, he looked up at her. "Please. Please." He put his hands up, but she sliced at them. Blood squirted out of him, staining the white tiles and porcelain. Her face was splattered with his blood. One crimson drop hung from her lip.

She straddled his feeble body and glared with a harrowing look. He didn't even recognize the woman he once knew in the face of this seething, raging lunatic. He made a feeble attempt to grab her wrists. "How could you betray me like this?"

"Betray you! This is not a betrayal. You can only be betrayed if you first trust. You don't know how to trust. You, my dear, are just getting what you deserve."

And with that, she released a bloodcurdling shriek and plunged the knife deep into his chest.

Noah struggled to take one last, short breath. As life drained from his eyes and the sight of her faded into darkness, a small breath escaped his mouth as he tried to form his last words. But she would never hear that final: "I still love you."

AFTERWORD

Thank you for reading *Noah's Story*. I am always grateful to those who take the time to read my writing. If you have not read *Circle of Betrayal* (the first book in the *Close Enough to Kill* series) and are interested in Kadee and Yvonne's side of the story, this book is told from multiple points of view and will give more insight into what it was like for each of them to be involved with Noah Donovan.

Also, the investigation into his murder is covered in the second half of *Circle of Betrayal*. I wrote this novella after readers had asked to know more about Noah and Belle. And honestly, as much as I had mixed feelings toward Noah before writing this book, I felt he had a right to tell his story. I'm glad he did, because I was quite affected by his narrative (I was exhausted from his emotions toward the end), and I learned more about a dynamic I have seen clinically. In some ways writing inside his head, gave me an unfiltered experience of the torment that men who have suffered these types of boundary betrayals, experience.

Although the story is entirely fictional, the dynamic between Noah and his mother, as disturbing as it is, is a very real phenomenon.

Sexual abuse is not exclusive to girls, nor does it always involve clear cut boundary violations such as penetration. The type of sexual abuse explored in this book is more subtle, and in some ways, because of the subtly, more damaging. As you can see from the narrative, Noah as a young boy struggles to reconcile knowing something isn't right between his mother and him, while also being excited by her visits. This is one of the things that make sexual abuse so damaging. There is a physical reaction, which leads to conflict and confusion. Many adult survivors report that they feel responsible in some way, saying things like, "I had an erection, and/or an orgasm. I must have wanted it." This leads to tremendous shame and guilt. And it is NOT their fault.

When this happens, between a mother and son, the boy once a man may have problems with his sexual and intimate relationships with women. The earliest experience and attachment to sexual and intimate longings may become a twisted, shame-ridden, guilt-ridden desire. As men, they are then, simultaneously aroused and disgusted.

Sigmund Freud talked about the Madonna-Whore Complex, describing it as: *"Where such men love they have no desire and where they desire they cannot love."* You may have heard of this before, even if you didn't know there was a psychological term for it.

I tried to show this through Noah's narrative. His desire for Kadee left him riddled with the same conflicts he had early on with his mother. The fact that he wanted her sexually, that he felt gripped by his desire for her, made him feel disgusted.

Interesting, while writing *Circle of Betrayal*, I had a sense of what Noah Donovan went through but still, I was angry at him for what he was doing to the women who trusted him. In this book, once exclusively in his head – alone, his story, his perspective, I felt a deep empathy for him.

If you are interested in learning more about boundary violations/sexual abuse against boys and the long term consequences and treatment, I highly recommend *Betrayed as Boys: Psychodynamic Treatment of Sexually Abused Men*, by Richard B. Gartner.

I also have patient case studies describing this in my non-fiction books, *In the Therapist's Chair* and *Bare: Psychotherapy Stripped*.

Readers have asked, "What's next?" now that the series is complete. I am considering (and most likely will) continuing Kadee's story, picking up from the end of *Circle of Truth*, the last book in the series. It likely will be called the *Kadee Carlisle* series. I also have an outline for a novella from the murderer's perspective from the *Close Enough to Kill* series.

Right now, I am writing my second romance novel. The first romance novel, the draft of which is complete, is going through the first round of content editing. In contrast to the exploration of darker aspects of human nature explored in the *Close Enough to Kill* series, this book is more hopeful – heartbreaking and uplifting, simultaneously, exploring relationships, love, loss, pride and choice. It's a story about protagonist Olivia, who (for complicated reasons), winds up torn between two loves, one from her past and one in the present. It is told from multiple points of view, giving insight into Olivia's experience, as well as, the men she is involved with. I loved writing it.

For information about my writing, updates on releases and giveaways, please sign up for my newsletter here: http://www.jsgunn.com/blog/

Also, I love reader feedback. Reviews on Amazon and Goodreads are always greatly appreciated. And please feel free to contact me through my website if you have any comments or questions. I always enjoy hearing from my readers. And thank you, again, for your interest in my work.

Acknowledgments

Thank you to my editor and longtime friend, Carlo DeCarlo, whose brilliant edits and time and commitment to my writing has made this book, as well as my others, possible. Your tireless creative collaborations and support are so important to me. Whenever I feel stuck on a plot point or lost in the middle of a story, like I'm in a swamp surrounded by weeds, you're able to pull me out and clear up what's keeping the creative process from flourishing. I know with one email or phone call to you, I will be clear on where I'm going. And besides, our pizza-chats are one of my favorite Friday night activities. Thank you for everything.

To my husband, Joseph Gunn, thank you, as always, for your ongoing support and for putting up with me when my mind is lost inside the imaginary world of my characters. Also, I am grateful for your creation of another fantastic book cover. To my father, Philip Simon, I am so thankful for your ongoing support. I know how lucky I am to have you. It means everything.

To my friends who have joined me on this journey, Melinda Gallagher, Mike Alonzo, Ross Kenyata Marshall, Lisa Vainieri Marshall and Tyla Loria. Thank you for reading, re-reading, providing feedback and letting me bounce ideas off of you. I especially appreciate your latitude and generosity in discussions where we talk as if my characters are real. They are, aren't they? Your time and support is greatly appreciated. I couldn't have done it without your help!

Thank you to all of my readers for taking the time to read my work, posting reviews and/or writing to me with feedback. It is because of your requests to hear more from Noah Donovan that I wrote *Noah's Story*. And I am so glad that I did. I am grateful to each and every one of you. Thank you.

About the Author

Jacqueline Simon Gunn is a Manhattan-based clinical psychologist and writer. She has authored two non-fiction books, and co-authored two others. She has published many articles, both scholarly and mainstream, and currently works as a freelance writer. With her academic and clinical experience in psychology, Gunn is now writing psychological fiction. Her *Close Enough to Kill* series, explores the delicate line between passion and obsession, love and hate, and offers readers an elaborate look into the mind of a murderer.

In addition to her clinical practice and writing, Gunn is an avid runner and reader. Gunn is currently working on multiple writing projects, including two romance novels.

OTHER BOOKS BY JACQUELINE SIMON GUNN

Non-Fiction
Bare: Psychotherapy Stripped (co-authored with Carlo DeCarlo)
Borderline Personality Disorder: New Perspectives on a Stigmatizing and Overused Diagnosis (co-authored with Brent Potter)
In the Long Run: Reflections from the Road
In the Therapist's Chair

Fiction
Circle of Betrayal (*Close Enough to Kill* series - Book 1)
Circle of Trust (*Close Enough to Kill* series - Book 2)
Circle of Truth (*Close Enough to Kill* series – Book 3)
What He Didn't See (*Close Enough to Kill* series – Novella)

Made in the USA
Middletown, DE
18 July 2017